THE ARCHITECT

RJ Spencer

authorHOUSE®

AuthorHouse™
1663 Liberty Drive
Bloomington, IN 47403
www.authorhouse.com
Phone: 1-800-839-8640

Published by AuthorHouse 12/17/2012

ISBN: 978-1-4772-9033-0 (sc)
ISBN: 978-1-477-2-9034-7 (e)

Library of Congress Control Number: 2012921722

Introduction:

For us, chairs were sex on legs.

The group sat in the neat little room. The chairs were configured in a round. Circular. So, everyone could see everyone else. Could hear everyone else. But there were rules.

The chairperson was in charge. What was said there in that room was to stay there. Statements were to be made personal, from a personal perspective, from a personal point of view. There was to be no giving of advice. No crosstalk or interruptions. No one was to be judged. Everyone was to be introduced by name only.

The chairperson, Wild Bill, stood and admitted on behalf of the group that we are all powerless. Powerless when it came to great design and great lines, and specifically when it came to architecture. He admitted that no power on earth could restore us to sanity. But we had tried. We had followed the rules, the commandments; we had made a fearless moral inventory of ourselves, of our lives. But it was not enough to get us to change, to stop thinking about great design. Not in our sleeping or waking hours. Yes, architecture ruled our lives.

We were there to admit to ourselves and to one another the exact nature of our wrong doings. To admit our shortcomings. To make a list of those we had harmed through our sickness. And through getting together to say out loud, "Yes, I had a problem." We were not saints. Not miracle workers. We were there to assist each other and do all we could to convince every last one of us to stay away from architectural magazines. Architectural book shops. We would agree not to travel to discover for ourselves the wonders of ancient or modern architecture. We would desist from blogging with others yet to be afflicted with "our disease."

Everyone in the room was searching out for the same thing. Redemption and the possibility of a new freedom. A new happiness without architecture in our lives. We were there to understand our past, not to regret it, not to shut the door on it completely, but to understand that it no longer ruled us.

We were hoping to know the meaning of the words serenity and peace, no matter how far down the scale they might have dropped. We all wished for the feeling of uselessness and self-pity to disappear. We all wanted our selfishness, our self-seeking, to vanish. We hoped economic insecurity would leave us and that one day soon we would intuitively know how to handle the situations that used to baffle us. We hoped to realize that the comfort of fellow sufferers would help us do what we could not do alone. Which was to exist without design, exist without The Architect.

On the wall directly behind Chairman Wild Bill were the slogans and prayers our group had come to rely on in times of madness, when reinforcement was the only thing left. They were there in bold black type. Helvetica bold to be exact. The words often drew all our eyes. And they stayed with us. Whenever we needed them, we could look up and recite them in our minds.

ONE DAY AT A TIME.

I AM RESPONSIBLE.

ONLY I CAN MAKE A DECISION TO WALK AWAY FROM A GREAT BUILDING.

A CHAIR IS A VERY COMPLICATED OBJECT. A SKYSCRAPER IS ALMOST SIMPLER!

ONE BUILDING IS TOO MUCH—ONE THOUSAND IS NOT ENOUGH!

ARCHITECTURE IS A DISEASE, AN ILLNESS.

GOD IS IN THE DETAILS!

LESS IS MORE.

I AM NOT UNIQUE.

ARCHITECTURE STARTS WHEN YOU CAREFULLY PUT TWO BRICKS TOGETHER. THERE IT BEGINS.

We had been building toward that day for a very long time. The day we all had to tell our story. Our personal story about The Architect. Yes, The Architect. The ruler of our lives. Let's not give him another name, because that's what we called him. The Architect. Those of you who have come across him will readily recognize him.

CHAPTER 1.

The Architect's Assistant.

Let me introduce myself. I am The Architect's assistant. It has not always been so. Just for the last few years. I was with him when he coined the phrase "Anyone with money can buy taste. It doesn't mean they have it. It just means they can afford it."

My name is Stanley. But call me the Assistant. First in my class at Stanford, on scholarship all the way. But it doesn't really matter, because I'm getting ahead of myself. It's not my turn.

Wild Bill was running the show. So stay with me, and when it gets complicated I'll explain in my own words.

Wild Bill stood in front of us in the room with no character and shuffled his feet. He stood in front of his secondhand armchair, the one with the sagging handles, the odd-length feet, the cracked and wrinkled vinyl. He stood and looked at the three of us. Seated. He looked through us. Looking shamefully at our cocoons, the cocoon's that housed us. The woolly, overstuffed, mass-produced armchair that looked like a fat pig on steroids. The plastic pink molded bucket turned into a stool. The recliner rocker that showed the staples that held together the its MDF (medium-density fiberboard) frame as it sagged and creaked under the weight of one of us. The sloth-like beanbag that slithered on the floor like a tired fat snake, a python that had over eaten and could not move to save its life. The once-famous theater seat that was cut from its brothers by a chain saw, soiled by melting chocolate and popcorn fingers, drenched in sweat and bodily fluids, its faded redness laughing at the watching world.

I'm the one responsible for setting up the group. Me. The Assistant. I collected us. I knew everyone there. Intimately. I knew that we had more than two things in common. One was that we would rather die than live with bad design. Two was that we all knew The Architect. Intimately.

Wild Bill ran the group because he was appointed chairman, and like all of us in the room, he understood exactly what a chair should be. And what we were sitting in were not chairs per se.

Let me explain. For some of you a chair might represent a stable surface to sit on. You might not care if it has three legs or four legs. It might even have arms. It might be able to hold one or two people. You might think chairs belong in lounge rooms. Or kitchens. Or on verandahs. Or in cinemas. Or in cars. You might think most chairs have wooden frames. High backs. Headrests. But for us chairs were sex on legs. A chair is architecture on a micro level. Chairs are pit stops for the body. Chairs are objects we use when we work. Eat. Sit. Drink. Relax. While we watch television. Watch a movie. A chair can be active. Passive. Or neutral. Chairs can be modern. Or they can be from Ancient Egypt. Or the Tang Dynasty. From a one-man factory in the Adirondacks or a team of robotic welders from Effuzi. A chair to everyone in that room was an exercise in considered ergonomics, taking into account the functionality of weight. Stackability. Foldability. And most importantly of all. Design.

A chair is a chair, is a seat. It might have an upright back. A slight recline. A massive recline. It involves the distribution of weight, not to the chair but to the sitter, the sitter's body. For example, a seat that is higher than normal that results in someone dangling their feet will increase the pressure on the undersides of the sitter's knees (popliteal fold). While a lower seat will most likely shift the sitter's weight to their seat bones (ischial tuberosities). While a reclining seat will shift weight to the sitter's back. Low backrests support only the lumber region. Shoulder-height backrests support the entire back and shoulders. Headrests support the head as well. Because sitting for a long time can mean the difference between comfort and stress. So a chair is not just a chair. Not to us. And it shouldn't be just a chair to you. Look around you. What height are the backs of your chairs? What recline do they have? Do you know? Of course you don't. So here's a quick bit of history.

The Renaissance changed the mighty chair from being a privilege of state to quickly becoming a standard item of furniture for those who could afford to buy it. It was then that the chair started to change and take on whimsy, reflecting the fashions of the hour. Chairs were even used for endowed professorships; yes, they were also known as chairs. And The Architect was about to receive his endowed professorship. But it was to be of a different kind. It was not going to be endowed by Stanford or Berkeley. It was to be in dollars, big fat healthy dollars. But it relied on the one thing the Big Corporation did not understand. It was going to rely on the chair The Architect was to be sat in.

I am going to stop Wild Bill's proceedings for a minute. I knew what he was going to say; I had lived through it with him. First I want to give you a small picture of The Architect and what a chair meant to him.

You see. A chair was anything but a chair, especially to The Architect. A fact obviously not known by the huge corporation who invited The Architect to talk about his first commercial project. A massive multistory office complex. A headquarters for The Corporation itself. The Architect had been guaranteed free rein, which is the only reason he even agreed to take the meeting. Oh, and for the dollars. I forgot the dollars. Silly me.

The Architect let me drop him off that day downtown. Just outside the Big Corporation's downtown office. And he was impressed. From the curb he appreciated the flowing lines of their current building. The fluid form. The sculptured sides that resembled a shining silver structure that rang with subtle volumetric gestures. But it was the gracious curving roof that really took his eye. Followed by the fluid force-field of horizontal louvers that seemed to move when graced by either light or shadow. It was this playful language of the façade that really tickled his fancy and made him feel confident to proceed with the meeting. That and the cohesive character of the building's internal structures that from the curb he could only imagine.

The Architect kissed me on the forehead before he headed inside. I was shocked. I froze right there on the sidewalk. I watched him walk away. Frozen I saw him disappear inside The Corporation's bowels, and all I could do was stand there. Frozen in time. And it almost cost me plenty. Plenty. Because I was just about to be booked. Wheels clamped. Towed away. And The Architect would have made me pay the fine had I not been able to talk myself out of it. Which I did. But this was not the real cost. Not the real disappointment. The day was to have many heartaches. The first was to hit The Architect. The second was to hit the Big Corporation. The third was to punish me for the Big Corporation's foolishness.

You see, when The Architect entered the mighty and cavernous foyer of the Big Corporation he was instantly assured he had made the right decision to take on this brief. He convinced himself that he had been foolish in the past to say no to every commercial project. He believed the grandness and size of the "players involved"—The Corporation, the thousands of tradespeople, the board, The Corporation's interior designers, and the three engineering companies he would have to deal with—would all contribute to give him less prominence and undermine his position. His position. As. As The Architect. But seeing the inside of the Big Corporation helped convince him that he had been wrong. See, architects are the new celebrity chef. The only difference is that architects have to go to University and be able to draw and calculate and have ideas blessed by God to be successful. While most celebrity chefs only need to be obnoxious to succeed. Sorry—food is not a deal breaker for me.

The Architect felt for all the right reasons like he had been asked to play the Big Game in the Big End of Town one last time, and this time he was ready to play. He was more than ready. He had convinced himself walking into that foyer that his life had already changed for the best, for the bestest. And by saying yes to this project he had already moved to a cloud close to God.

The Architect made reception aware of his presence. They asked him to sit on a long, deep brown, distressed, Italian leather, four-person sofa. The type that Antonio Citterio would have designed in the late.seventies. You see, Antonio also trained as an architect at the Politecnico of Milan, Italy, but instead of designing houses he chose to design Chairs. Albeit long ones. The Architect sat himself down. Squirming his behind in the soft squeaky leather. Sitting back so his spine was fully supported. His feet touched the ground. His knees were perfectly bent at right angles. He thought to himself that Antonio might just have designed this sofa for The Architect because it fitted so perfectly. He was as happy as Larry sitting there. Smelling the scent of success that spewed from the air-conditioners with the ferocity of a thousand aromatic candles burning under his nose. He was momentarily intoxicated.

That was until the Bigwigs of The Corporation came down and introduced themselves. They were all smiles. All crease-proof suits. Beautiful white starched shirts. Big bold ties that were actually stylish and designed with taste. Their shoes were shiny. And black. It was the color of wealth. Black.

The Architect could smell himself being one of them. All he needed to do was sign the contract. One scrawny signature and he would be just like them. Except for the tie. The Architect thought he might wear a "'kerchief'." Or a cravat. Or a biker's headband. That he would wrap into a tube-like vessel and tie around his neck. Because inside he really was a rebel; it's just that no one knew it. He thought he would even buy the crudest. Most "'fuck- off'" biker headbands in the hope that someone might one day be able to read the sentiment printed on it. When they were looking closer than they should. Whilst they were imagining themselves in The Architect's shoes. The headband might say "'Bikers Like To Fuck Big Girls'." Or, "'Your Wife's a Slut; I know, Because I Fucked Her'."

Yes, The Architect was in his Corporation heaven.

The Bigwigs from The Corporation shuffled him through the massive foyer. Gloating about the green design points as they walked. Rattling off celebrity names and brands of windows. Titanium metals. Leather floor tiles. Work done by craftsmen that only the super-rich could afford. The Bigwigs touched a hidden lever in a wall of solid oak and magically the wall moved. Open sesame.

The Bigwigs escorted The Architect into one of their most secret meeting rooms. Instantly The Architect beamed with pride. Instantly his face lit up. Instantly. Without even thinking he blurted out the words, "The chairs. They're mine. My design. What great taste you have."

The Architect moved toward one of the chairs. Fondling it. Feeling each join and crevice. Dexterously handling each rib. Each leg. Running his ten fingers around each curve. But something was wrong. He started to fumble with the chair. He was asked to sit down but silently refused. The others had already taken their places. But The Architect was intent on overturning the chair and laying it upside down on the mahogany inlaid table. He inspected the frame, looking for the marking that would guarantee the authenticity of his design. The factory. The stamp of approval. But it was not there. So he overturned another. Then the next. He pulled one Bigwig at a time out of their chair so he could overturn them one by one until he had inspected each one thoroughly.

And it was done. Without a conscious thought he called them "Fucking whores who bleed the integrity of genius to look like they have taste, like they can afford taste. But they do it at the designer's expense. Fucking corporate whores."

And with that The Architect walked out. He walked away from his cloud closer to God. Away from his shiny black shoes and his biker headbands. He walked straight out and never considered taking a commercial project ever again.

Yes, all three of us were set to suffer sooner or later. The Architect. The Big Corporation. And me. But I digress. Let's go back to hear what Wild Bill had to say when he finally stopped shuffling his feet, as he was now ready to address his little gathered group sitting in our cocoons.

"I welcome you here tonight as chairman. And I will admit on all our behalves that we are powerless over architecture. That our lives have become unmanageable. Otherwise we wouldn't be here."

"Here, here" came the cheer from us all.

"We are about to admit in front of each other that we are powerless when it comes to great design. Great materials. Great manufacturing. We are all about to acknowledge that the only power greater than ourselves, greater than The Architect, is God, and only he can restore our normality. We have all made a conscious decision to turn our lives over to that greater power. We have all made a searching and fearless moral inventory of ourselves and our mental possessions. We are about to admit to ourselves, to the others in this room, the exact nature of our wrongs. And we pray that these defects will be removed from our lives—but not before we all have the opportunity to tell our own story. This is our chance to speak so we can finally be free. I remind you once more we are all under oath. Under the oath of God. And that everything said can and will be used against us. Let me start by acknowledging for all of us that if it had not been for The Architect, none of us would be here today.

"Bruce, I call on you to stand here in front. In front of the group and tell us your story. Without a lie. Without an over exaggeration. Tell us the truth, the whole truth, and nothing but the truth."

Chapter 2.

Bruce.

Bruce stood. A shy man. Small for his age. I know it's a strange thing to say—small for his age—but for all of Bruce's forty-nine years Bruce still looked like he needed his nose wiped and his lunch box packed. After all, Bruce brought this whole thing on himself. You see, Bruce pursued The Architect for months to convince him to take on his piss small project. But The Architect did it. And it is amazing. The most amazing small plot, small-space house in the country.

You see, The Architect was one of the great small architects in the land. Small because he only ever took on residential commissions, even before The Corporation fucked him over. Fucked him over before they even kissed.

The Architect accepted commissions from some of the country's top celebrities. He also turned down more than he took on. But every now and then he dedicated himself to taking on poor cases. Cases where he could totally impose his own vision. Cases where he could control the entire build. To build the house he would want for himself with other people's money. But how many houses could one have? In Bruce's case it was one.

"Hi, I'm Bruce. And I'm a design junkie."

The three of us cheered. And stomped our feet. Yelling our reassurance.

"Well done, Bruce."

"Love you, Bruce."

"Tell it like it is, Bruce."

"We're here for you, Bruce."

Sure it was false. It was fake support. Bruce didn't mind, though. It comforted him. Soothed him. As he was the first to stand and bare his ass to us.

Bruce continued. "I've been a design junkie since I can remember. I remembered my mother telling me exactly what my name—Bruce—meant. It meant origin, original. So Bruce was original. And I wanted everything from that day that was not the same as anyone else. I wanted to Brucify it. To make it mine. To make it me."

We all cheered.

"I saved every last dollar I earned. I piled it in the bank. Managed it. Invested it. I watched it grow and wondered what I might buy with it. What I might buy that would stamp my originality, my Bruceness. I didn't want a watch; everyone has a watch. But not everyone has a plane. I looked at the Harmony LSA by Evektor, an amazing light sport aircraft. A two-seater. But unless I flew it to air shows and showed it off to the rich and famous, no one would know I had it. I didn't fly by the way, because I didn't like air travel; I was also scared of heights. So I looked at cars. I searched out every one-off car maker. Every kit specialist. I tracked down every engine configuration I could find until I had the specifications for the world's only Bruce car. But I didn't like to drive much; I liked to take public transport. It was then I that I found my calling. My Bruceness. I found real estate. Land to be precise. Having land was a feeling unlike any other. I could walk on it. Kick the dirt that lay on it. Camp on it. Sit on it. Sleep on it. No one could take it away from me. Steal it from me. I owned a small piece of the world, and I was ecstatic. It was then that I realized I wanted shelter on it. Not your average shelter. I wanted a statement."

Bruce then proceeded to tug at his groin. His underpants, to be precise, as they constantly seemed to be imbedded in his ass, and no amount of finger pulling could satisfactorily dislodge them.

"I did my research when it came to wanting to build my first home. My first and last home. After all I had saved for over forty years. So I called The Architect. I had been following him ever since he won the National Architecture Award for Residential Designs for his building 'piece Da Stink."

Sorry, it's me again, the Assistant. I have to interrupt. I know it seems rude, but it was then that Bruce showed exactly what a turd he really was. He pulled from under his jacket a copy of the article about The Architect from the *Architectural Digest Annual*. It was bad enough that Bruce had the article; it was ridiculous that Bruce had had the article laminated. But not before he used his green highlighter to feature the adjectives used to describe how wonderful The Architect and "piece Da Stink" really was. The words used included stupendous … exalting … wondrous … awe-inspiring … astonishing … astounding … breathtaking … staggering … and that was just the first sentence.

Either way. You get it. The Architect was good. And by good I mean really good. So instead of listening to Bruce while he Brucifies everything, let me recall for you the day Bruce came into The Architect's office.

It was a Monday. Nine zero one a.m. Yes, Bruce had the decency to wait one minute before he walked into the office. But Bruce did not come alone; he came with bags of architecture books. Scribbles. Torn articles. Sorry, nothing was in fact torn; they were all beautifully cut pages of reference material. Plus he had cutouts of every house and article The Architect had been featured in.

All this for a house "two point six meters by four meters."

Yes, Bruce had saved his whole life to build a micro home. The beauty of the idea was that it was to be built four hours from the nearest town or neighbor in the middle of the desert. So that's what stopped The Architect in his stride. I remember him asking Bruce to tell him more.

As Bruce poured out his heart, revealing his inadequacy as a human being. The Architect realized that Bruce did in fact need to live four hours from the rest of the world. Just so he could be appreciated. Appreciated by the solemn quiet of loneliness. Appreciated by the vacant space around him. By the ever-present wind that burned in summer and chilled to the bone in winter. Appreciated by the ever-changing sky and the never-changing landscape. Yes, Bruce had picked the perfect private location for his micro home because he was that pathetic.

In the one minute while Bruce continued to speak and waffle, The Architect had begun the design, drawn across a piece of perfectly white, crease-proof paper. It sat there like it was levitating. A low-slung modernist box. It was time for Bruce to leave so The Architect could experiment with the subtle manipulation of scale and proportion. So The Architect could rattle through the articulation of building details and distinguish himself again at someone else's expense.

The Architect walked away from Bruce. Just walked away. He laid out the fine-line drawing and started speaking to himself. It sounded like he was speaking in tongues. But he wasn't. It was just a ploy he used to separate himself from the rest of us mortals.

I watched Bruce as he collected all his bits of paper one by one. Filing them into their rightful place in his accordion folder. He was about to walk up to The Architect, to continue his boring recantation of his personal history. The scattered facts about his upbringing, and information about his desert site when I intercepted him. I manhandled him to sign the no-call, no-speak privacy document that forbade Bruce from discussing anything about his project with anyone but The Architect and myself.

"That's it for today, Bruce. We'll be in touch. Bye."

And with my help Bruce was gone. It was now I had time to watch the master at work.

At times like this The Architect was accustomed to me sitting behind him on a raised stool specially designed by me that let me see him work. To see his drawing process. His thinking process. It was at times like these that I would recite with him his speaking of tongues. The Architect and I would repeat his chant … the body of which I had written down one word at a time just to make out exactly what he was saying. I am not certain if the rant was original or if he copied it. But it went something like this:

"We have reached the end of a decade and a half in which digital computation has given architects new creative opportunities to access the geometrical space opened up by post-seventeenth-century mathematicians. The resulting new wave of interest in the relationship of mathematics to space making has been aesthetically driven, and yet its expression has transcended the metaphorical. It has found expression from within the process of making as a new species of

13

architecture and has infiltrated architecture in ways that have forged radical change. What are the philosophical impulses that have led architecture to embrace mathematical thought anew?"

And he and I would repeat it. Several hundred times if necessary. Until the first draft of the design was complete.

You see, living with an architect-designed house is a great privilege. The thing about living with great design is that it does push you. It forces you to come to terms with it. It doesn't come to terms with you. It keeps you thinking about things. How would this look there? Does that style go or not? And like it or not, no matter how hard he would try, Bruce would be the one element that would not go with The Architect's amazing design. And Bruce would never understand why. Not till the day he died. Bruce was also a first timer. A virgin. Some of The Architect's customers were astute about architects. They would watch them come out of college and start their practices and then grab them at the start of their careers. When their drive was at its maximum. Their costs at their minimum. A steal really. And when they became famous their house was far more valuable than they could imagine.

Wild Bill was one such client. This guy came back for more even after The Architect was famous. But again I digress—there will be plenty of time to hear from and speak about Wild Bill.

CHAPTER 3.

The Hummingbird.

I watched The Architect put pencil to paper for Bruce in waves of finely articulated movement. Movement so precise. So free hand. So fluid. He was indeed the hummingbird of architecture.

This was my favorite part. The part I looked forward to. You see, The Architect could actually draw; in truth, he sketched, and even he had his rules. There was to be no CAD drawing on the computer. The Architect was all about the rapid execution of freehand drawing to record his ideas. It was never to be a finished work. It was just part of the process. He could have drawn on the back of an envelope, a napkin, a cigarette packet. But that was not The Architect's style. No. His platform had to be pristine and white, even if it was superseded along the design path. This initial concept sketch would become a piece of the central idea. It was part of his freedom-of-thought process. The time when he had the most freedom. Before he committed it to a scale drawing. Which, in fact, was my job.

So we chanted. Spoke in tongues. And I was swept up watching the hummingbird.

The fine black pencil marks clearly showed The Architect's intellect. Each time he drew across a white void he showed a brain wave in action. It was like watching a human lie-detector machine at work. Fine slender black lines were drawn against an endless background of white, but as they aggregated they became something new. Something newborn. These lines ended the qualities of ambiguity. They were a reality to his imagination, fine and precise. The lines seemed to know exactly where to go. Where to start and where to stop. How to sit next to the line beside them. How to sit above the line below them. The lines knew how to amalgamate with each other to create The Architect's vision.

The Architect designed for Bruce a low-slung box that hugged the earth around it. Standing on its own four feet, like space module posts embedded lightly in the moon's surface. In fact the legs were anodized aluminum reinforced with titanium. They secretly went three meters into the desert earth, but no one could tell. For the observed, they seemed to be tiptoeing on the desert dirt. The box itself was long and skinny. It was a mere 266 cm wide. It ran north-south. But it was big enough to house a double bed measuring 198 cm x 107 cm. Storage space for bedding. Cleaning equipment. A sliding table that would accommodate up to three people. A flat- screen television in the living/dining space. Shower and toilet cubicle. The kitchen area featured a double hob, sink and extending tap, microwave, fridge and freezer unit, a three-compartment waste unit. Storage shelves. Cutlery drawers with gentle return-sprung sides. And, double-level work surfaces to save space. There was thermostat-controlled ducted heating and air-conditioning. Plus the mandatory fire and smoke detectors. Not that anyone would hear the scream of alarm or Bruce's scream if the place were set on fire. Being hours away meant the fire detectors were just for Bruce.

The outside skin was again representative of a lunar module. Shiny, ever-reflective stainless steel covered parts with a matte finish while other sections had highly polished mirror-like panels.

The Architect's design called for an industrial steel canopy that shielded the entire house from the brutal summer desert sun. There was a six-foot gap between the house and the steel canopy. The void that was pure genius. It allowed the resident breeze to pass through it, keeping things cool. And when night fell, bringing with it a massive and rapid drop in temperature, the canopy stopped the warmth from escaping. The outside skin reflected the sun as well, blinding any flying object within a kilometer of it. It was energy efficient. This was combined with the solar photovoltaic system that housed a small-diameter vertical axis wind generator, and presto. Daytime power was diverted into the grid while nighttime power was provided by the wind turbine and reserve batteries. There were two times in a day when it was seventy degrees in the desert. The Architect designed the house to be at that temperature at all times.

Bruce's house had space-age wall and roof insulation. A west-facing overhang to block the hot afternoon sun in summer. I could list every design element The Architect incorporated. Every recycling point. But you get the picture.

The most important feature The Architect employed was the one point he never told Bruce about. The Architect had hard-wired cameras and remote control units into his design just so he could periodically check on Bruce to make sure he was respecting his design. You see, The Architect made every client sign a legal document to say they would not. Could not. Change one thing about their own home without the direct approval of The Architect. And if The Architect deemed their request was not fitting, then their request would not happen. That's just the way things were.

With a flourish and the release of the pencil, the hummingbird walked away from the table without a word. Finished.

It was now dark. The Architect dressed himself in his overcoat and scarf and walked out of the office as if a gust of wind had just left. Now it was my turn. It was time for the detail drawings. That was my job. The Architect had written with great precision the sizes of rooms. Ceiling height. Bench heights. Window frames. And it was my job to draw them perfectly to scale. I had the night to show one and all, and The Architect, how the component parts fit together. Then I would do section drawings to highlight the construction details, to show the complex junctions. My favored scale for the drawings was 1/5. Luckily it was also The Architect's. I think this alone got me the job.

CHAPTER 4.

My (The Assistant's) Job Interview.

How could I ever forget meeting The Architect for the first time? It was like meeting God. He knew I had finished first in my class; I guess that's what attracted him to me. Attracted in a strange way. Because all he was attracted to was excellence. I remember meeting him in his nondescript office. His outgoing assistant showed me in and gave me the task, and I had five minutes to finish it. I had to name the twenty most prolific residential architects in the world as voted for by the international architect panel that had assembled in Paris the summer before. I had read the article almost twenty times the very day it had been published in *Architecture World*. But today I froze. Yes, froze. I could not think of one of them. Not one. But I could see all of their work. So I started to draw. Freehand. And wildly. I started to draw twenty residential buildings. I could see them as if they were projected onto the page. Their sleek lines. Their impossible curves. Their rooflines. The ones imbedded under tons of soil and grass. The ones perched on a mountain. The ones constructed on a miniature plot of land in a laneway of a massive city. I remember handing them to the assistant. Who was not so impressed. I remember waiting silently. With not a sound from the enclosure housing The Architect, I sat there for what seemed like hours until the assistant walked out, leaving the door open. I looked and listened until I could wait no longer. I walked up to the door, knocking while I looked in, my eyes searched for the rays of sunlight that must shroud such a luminary. But all I could find was a meek. Small-framed man. With perfectly trimmed hair. Perfectly fitted clothes, all designer but not gaudy. He wore perfectly groomed leather slip-on shoes. He must have sensed me, because he spoke just before I was about to stutter my words.

"You did not know one name. Not one. But you remembered all their designs. You're hired. You start Monday. I come in at 8:45. I expect you to be in before me. Have my coffee ready. Make sure it's not too hot. Have the day's paper on my desk. And search daily for the most concealed miniature camera systems you can find. I want 1920 x 1080 resolution. See you Monday."

And with that I was hired.

Monday came too fast. I had not slept properly as Monday's dawn approached. I had tossed and turned with stomach pains all night. It was 4:44 when I got up. Have you ever noticed how the numbers on the digital clock randomly make or include the number eight? Well they do, mostly. So I rose and showered. I remembered not to wear cologne as instructed. I decided to eat as I glanced at the clock. It was exactly 5:18 as I raised my spoon. See, I told you. I could stomach just three or four mouthfuls. So I decided to go into the office early.

I remembered the alarm code (four eight three six—see, eight is in everything) and sat in the dark by myself and memorized everything. Everything in its perfect place. Everything in perfect order. I looked until I remembered as much as I could. I forget to tell you that I have a photographic memory. So everything would remain in its place. I would not get it wrong. That's how I could draw every design by the top twenty. It is something I did not tell The Architect. It was something I was going to keep safe. Keep close, and use to show off when I needed to. Having said that, I was never sure why I could not remember the names of the architects but I could remember their drawings. Must be a glitch in the photograph somewhere.

I started to look closely at The Architect's files. They were all alphabetically perfect right down to apostrophes. I fingered the files with my eyes. *A*s turned into *D*s and then into *R*s, and then I spotted a name I knew. A name I had read. Could it be Wild Bill? I gingerly moved my hand forward and was just about to grab hold of it when I heard the front door open. I pretended to be dusting the filing cabinet as The Architect walked in and went straight to his desk. He was early. It was just 8:30. See, again an eight. I closed the cabinet without a single sound. It was something I could safely do as I noticed all the hinges had been oiled so they moved without a sound. I presumed the other assistant had worked that out. I asked if The Architect would like his coffee early. He graced me with a smirk that said not. Eight forty five it was to be. And it was.

I went to the coffee shop as directed. I ordered as I was told. One coffee for The Architect please. The barista smiled and moved from his workstation. He moved to a place under the shop shelf. A place kept only for The Architect. The coffee he handled was single origin, the beans from trees grown in the shade, on a hilltop, four thousand meters above sea level. The coffee cherries were picked by hand to ensure only the ripe cherries were chosen. The Architect's coffee was Nicaraguan Maragogype. When I came back with the coffee. In a double cup. Double insulated. The outside shell wrapped in a serviette just like I was told. I watched The Architect as he cautiously sipped it, not wanting to burn his tongue. After testing it he swigged his coffee with gusto. I sighed. I moved away to my desk and sat there doing nothing. Until he called me over.

"Come. Sit behind me. Just don't get too close, and don't make any noise at all. None."

I stood and watched him. He was working on a home of immense grandeur. Money was again buying style. And order. And design excellence. I watched as his fingers nursed the pencil like a soft piece of plasticine. He neither fingered it nor dented it. Nor did he take it for granted. He let it warp against his hand. He held it like it was precious. Which in his grip. It was.

I had been on my feet for three hours. So I made a mental note to myself to wear more comfortable shoes tomorrow. Or at least insteps.

I watched and called to memory everything The Architect drew until my stomach rumbled. The Architect stopped. He did not turn around. But he did order me to eat something before I returned to my submissive position. Which I did instantly.

I made a second note to myself to work out an eating system, a system that had me eating at every break in his drawing regime so it would not happen again. I also decided to design a viewing chair so I could sit instead of stand while I spend hours watching the master.

When The Architect had gone home that night I Googled

the name on the client form The Architect had been working on. It was him. I guessed it. I recalled how famous this client was. It was an earlier life. His earlier life that let him see fame. Wild Bill was an NFL hero. But now I knew him by a very different name—John Shepherd. It was evidently his real name. But no one would ever call him that. Only The Architect, I presumed.

I remember seeing Wild Bill in the flesh for the first time recently. It was as Chairman Wild Bill, and even at our first meeting he impressed me. Impressed me with his physical stature. He was a big man. But knowing him for even a short time I understood that he was not going to be a match for The Architect. Not even with his bulk.

Yes, The Architect was a worthy opponent for anyone. Had his physical attributes matched his intellect, The Architect would have been an even more formidable opponent than he already was. But this was not a match to be decided by strength.

The home for Wild Bill (aka Chairman Wild Bill) was palatial to say the least. Extravagant. Unnecessary. Over stated. It screamed everything that people who fall into money seem to scream. It screamed, "Look at me. Look how big my dick is. Look how much money I have." And it screamed, "*Fuck you,*" to all you have-nots, the ones who only dreamed of owning something so pretentious.

Yes, Wild Bill had an illustrious career in college, from humble beginnings to the pros, and he spent money. Lavished money on his posse. He also had an agent who invested in commercial real estate for him, making him rich. As an older man he went to college to study law. He met The Architect by coincidence. Introduced by a friend. And later in life when he was even more successful, he gave him money, as much as he wanted, so The Architect would design him a house.

Then Wild Bill did the unimaginable. He sold it and

came back for more. Yes, Wild Bill flaunted money in The Architect's face and asked for another house! Wild Bill explained that his ex-wife's partner had purchased the house and Wild Bill wanted him to build another bigger, better house on the same street as his ex-wife's house. Two of The Architect's houses in the same street?

It caused The Architect some pain. He only had so many hours in his life. To design again for the same client? It came down to the dollars of persuasion. But I will come back to Wild Bill. My legs are aching.

CHAPTER 5.

The Viewing Chair.

I had to design my viewing chair to save my legs while I watched the hummingbird. And I had to make it impressive. I would be judged. I knew it.

I opted for a molded chair. Lightweight. From a resourceful material. It had to flow. Like water over a rock. Like a cushion under my torso. It had to make a statement. To myself and The Architect.

It was like my first self-imposed test. I wanted to impress the world with its design. So the first night I drew. I formulated. I played with curves. I decided on plywood as my timber of choice. But not any plywood. It had to be marine ply. And layers of it. And rather than hide the plywood with paint or stain, I was determined to highlight the natural beauty of finely sanded wood. The flexible ply was to lay with the grain, perpendicular to the grain of the next layer separated by a black glue line. The alternating light and dark wood from sustainable trees would be covered by a clear lacquer finish to seal the deal. I researched the flow of water over sharp angles and memorized the curves. What people could do with rubber, I would do with timber. The final result would suck up under my butt, setting me above the master as I watched fully supported. Able to concentrate on his wrist. Reading his thoughts just after he had them.

It was to take me a week at least to design and build it. So in preparation for the following day I needed to practice my stand. At home I stood to draw. Stood to read. To eat. I stood every minute of every day until my legs got used to it. I trained the muscles that supported my upper body to stop lower-back pain and to stop my spine taking the brunt of the pressure, so my torso would take the majority of the strain. So my soles would get used to my constant weight. I trained my insteps to stretch and recoil. I stood with my head up straight. Chin in. Without tilting my head forward or backward or sideways. I made sure my earlobes were in line with the middle of my shoulders. Shoulder blades back. Chest forward. Knees straight. Stomach tucked in. The arches of my feet supported.

I stood alongside my computer after sketching my design for my viewing chair. After searching out the timber supplier closest to my house. After sourcing the nearest boat builder. After getting everything in order.

I then stood and Googled the historical background of Wild Bill. I wanted see what kind of man he was. Then work out, like my chair design, what made him become Chairman Wild Bill.

CHAPTER 6.

Wild Bill.

The research files said that Wild Bill was a hero to a town. To the NFL. To a nation.

Before I made my first mental sketch of Wild Bill, I had to Google and work out exactly what a hero was. It said a hero inspires others and benefits others by their actions and by their accomplishment, against all odds, not letting anything get between them and their dream. A hero fights because it's the only thing he or she knows how to do. A hero also learns by his or her mistakes.

It seems Wild Bill was such a hero. Born January 25, 1956. Poor by money standards. Rich in natural talent. Schooled in the life of hard knocks. Graduated from Oklahoma. Then UCLA. Wild Bill was awarded and named an All-American, winner of the Davey O'Brien Award for the best college quarterback of the year. After college he went straight into the NFL draft. The jock was the first overall pick and became a legend. He led his team to three Super Bowl championships. But that's not what made him a hero. What made him a hero was his compassion for those off the field. He never had any compassion for those going head to head with him. Never gave an inch. But for those sick, especially those children who were suffering, he could not do enough. Could not give enough. If it was a smile, an autograph, a kidney, or a check, it was all he could do. Wild Bill started the after-game drive to get members of every team on the phone after every game to take calls from fans. Sick fans. The ones unable to watch the game in the stadium. It was before the Internet. It was before doing a good deed made you famous.

After he had such an illustrious career, everyone thought Wild Bill would become a commentator; surely it was all mapped out for him. But he decided that it was time to go into a new game. He decided on being Chairman Wild Bill. Yes, there were people to help, and I was one of them. And that's why I am guessing he is Chairman Wild Bill now. We, his sick children, gathered before him, waiting in the room for him to sign his autograph and magically fix us all. But a signature even on a big fat check was not going to be enough to fix any of us. In all honesty, it was his meeting with The Architect that changed him. In ways he would never have imagined.

Going through The Architect's files I confirmed it with the photo—it was Wild Bill and his second wife. He must have been around thirty-eight years old. He was standing as proud as punch outside his first new home. And right next to him, in his shadow, was a much younger Architect. He was standing almost shyly, almost as if he had been included in the photograph by mistake. His hands were wringing each other out like a dishcloth. His face was tilted down as if trying to hide his identity. His right foot was halfway hidden behind his left. His facial expression gave it away. He was not impressed. Not by the house he designed. He was wasting time standing for photos when he could be designing.

So the chairman was Wild Bill and Wild Bill was the chairman.

Now all I had to do was find the finished photographs of Wild Bill's second new house. The documentation of its design and actual realization in photographic form was too valuable to be destroyed. Too important to be left on show. It must be hidden. In pride of place.

Knowing how much The Architect prided himself on his pencil-ship I knew he would keep a copy of everything. I searched the cupboards. The boxes. Nothing. I turned everything inside out. Took out and replaced things in exactly the same position. I took photos on my phone to double-check that I had replaced things perfectly. I had rifled the entire office and was keen to see what I had missed. I plugged my phone into my laptop so I could download the photos and lock them away under password protection before erasing them from my phone. I loaded them and blew them up. Going over each shot with a magnifying glass. I spotted it on my third run through. A USB. Stuck. Hidden in fact, in a small chamber inside the main drawing desk.

I put the USB drive into my computer. Copied it. And I returned it exactly as it was meant to be. I even did it with gloves on just in case The Architect regularly tested things for foreign fingerprints.

It loaded like any other file. No password needed. It opened and showed itself for what it was, a place of magnificence. Lavish. Plush. Overstated wealth. But in a nice kind of way, because it had all the hallmarks of The Architect; it had his refined lines. And it had that "power of place." It could have been designed for an industrialist. But it was designed for an ex-jock, Wild Bill, and his second wife, Trophy.

I checked out every detail of the house, matching plan against the accompanying photographs of the finished product. There were over two hundred images. I studied them. Gushed at them. The walls were surfaced in frescoed plaster. It was more like a Renaissance chapel than an airy modern loft (read a large open space used for residential use). The library was den-like, of course. Hanging over the living area was the master bedroom. Perched high above. Like an opera balcony. Wild Bill called it his eagle's nest. A proud place that only the few shall inhabit. It was on show for all to see. But for none to occupy. Or so Wild Bill thought.

It was then that I noticed the inconsistency. It was not an innocuous error. It was intentional. It showed up in every room. The same detailed sphere. There were multiple in some rooms. Ten in the eagle's nest. I went through the drawings just to confirm their presence. And they were. Small perfectly round spheres on every blueprint, added by The Architect. Every tiny drawing had one at least. They were hidden cameras. Like the ones I had researched. Small. Undetectable. Perfect. With 1920 x 1080 resolution.

It seemed that Wild Bill had agreed that The Architect would install multiple hidden cameras in every room. Hidden cameras. Cameras with no red or green pilot light. Cameras that recorded twenty-four hours a day. Cameras that were motion sensitive. Cameras that went back to a hard drive for storage. Wild Bill paid a fee for an operative to watch the tapes and report back. He had been given his instructions and knew what he was looking for. *But why?* you ask. You will soon find out.

Not right away, but eventually I became the operative myself, and my job was to keep an eye on Trophy. She was much younger than Wild Bill. Beautiful. A peach ready for picking. And Wild Bill had picked her. He wanted her protected. He also wanted her watched. There was to be no third party in the eagle's nest. Ever. So I watched. I also researched. Trophy had been an ugly duckling at school, but her ugly duckling syndrome gave her life gifts. Her self-esteem had been low all her teenage life, and Wild Bill wanted it kept that way. But the low self-esteem also gave her a good heart, a shy personality, and a wonderful soul. Her sense of humor was great, although disguised. And Wild Bill wanted all those things kept that way.

It was as if Wild Bill had found Trophy just as she blossomed into beauty. Before she had time to realize that she was attractive. Popular. Lusted after. Before she realized who she was. And Wild Bill wanted it kept that way.

On watching the cameras I was often distraught with Wild Bill's actions. The way he treated her. I showed The Architect. He took it in his stride, never commenting. But I could tell he was not happy. I recorded that unhappiness.

Chapter 7.

The Architect Is Cranky.

"That day" was the first day when I could remember that The Architect was late. I had his coffee at the perfect temperature. His papers unfolded and stacked just as he liked them. I was ready, and I sat on my perched stool and waited. I sat and looked around the office. Nothing was out of place. Nothing. I edged toward the end of my stool one hundred times, thinking about heading straight for the locked confidential files to see if there were more secret files alongside those of Wild Bill's. But every time I started to move I imagined a sound. It could have been the sound of The Architect. But it wasn't. And I didn't have the guts to do it. I thought about calling him on his cell phone, but he never gave me his number. So I sat and waited until the tornado entered the room. The swearing and cursing entered the room eight feet (see, it's the number eight again) before his body entered. To save you from being disappointed with The Architect and to save you from The Architect's rant, I will keep the gory details and bad language for another time. The matter for concern was The Corporation.

It seemed that The Corporation had been interviewed about their new headquarters. It had been a glowing report. It named the highly successful architect who would be heading the project, a former classmate of The Architect. Someone who had not achieved the success The Architect had. The Corporation had said, and I quote, "The Corporation had scoured the known design planet and hand-selected the very best candidate in the world for this project. The project will set new standards for design. For construction. For creative interpretation of New Architecture."

"New Architecture," The Architect growled. "'New fucking architecture. Who do these assholes think they are?"

He went on to read the article line by line. Never asking if I was interested. Only presuming—and he was right—that I had to hear every word. Process every emotion he spewed forth.

The article was titled "Corporations Are the Medicis of the Twenty-First Century" and ranted about corporations leading the architectural charge. The Architect spewed that he would force them to write a follow-up article titled "Let Them Eat Shit." I made a mental note. He continued, explaining that the new headquarters of The Corporation was to be built from titanium, chrome, gold and silver. Lined in moonstone. And it was to be the first international headquarters to be built in the middle of a lake. A fucking lake. Accessible only by water. By boat. By private gondola. And with that The Architect tore the newspaper to shreds. To small, tiny pieces of random type that fell next to one another on the floor, making no-sense at all. Making nonsense words that were not in any dictionary. Words like "deium," "romeT," "doonst," "eadq," "Glensive," "keTh." Stupid words that would not fit in the language of even a moron. Words that lay on the floor staring at me like diamonds glistening in the sun. I was mesmerized by them until I heard his scream. He screamed at me to gain my attention. The attention I gave him every second of every day except now. He screamed at me to source every contractor and tradesman employed to work on The Corporation's new headquarters. He said to do whatever it took to get their names and profiles. Their backgrounds. Their financial details. To document the limit of their work on the project. To list all the suppliers of materials. Every fucking bit of it. I knew exactly what I had to do, and I knew who to get to help me. An old acquaintance. But first there was today's business. Bruce was coming in. And I had also left Bruce stranded in front of the group for a while now in the tiny little room that was getting hot. Let's get back to Bruce and his story.

Chapter 8.

Back to Bruce in the Round.

Wild Bill didn't so much as look at Bruce standing feebly before the group—he studied him in a way that frightened me. I knew what Wild Bill was capable of. Bruce had no idea, and he cared even less. All he knew was that his stunning low-slung micro home was haunted in a way he could never explain.

While Wild Bill studied Bruce's face and watched his mouth contort and stammer in front of the group as he spoke. He also watched Bruce shuffle and tried to gauge via his body language what pained Bruce. He watched Bruce paw at his underwear as Bruce made nonsense of his story. Yes, Bruce was unable to explain in ordinary words what had happened. It could have been he was reliving the fear he felt entering his own home. Whatever it was, I'll explain on Bruce's behalf, or else Bruce's convoluted story will take forever.

As I touched on, The Architect designed Bruce a magnificent box. A box that housed its own ghost. A ghost that recorded every move Bruce made. That recorded every shit Bruce took. Every wank Bruce had. It recorded every microwave meal Bruce overcooked. Yes, every waking moment. You see, The Architect originally installed hidden cameras in every house he designed so he could check up on his clients. Check that they did not alter or disturb any of his design elements. And that went right down to the choice of paint color. You see, clients like Bruce might have paid for their houses, but The Architect owned the IP. He made them sign it away from the very beginning. It might be theirs, the actual house, but it was also his. The design integrity was his. Maybe it was Wild Bill who gave him the idea. Or maybe not.

The cameras in Bruce's home had no light. No pilot glow to give the game away. They were powered by the same solar cells that heated and cooled Bruce's house. They recorded right onto a hard drive in The Architect's office. An office hidden behind a secret door, that no one knew about. No one but The Architect and me. Originally The Architect anticipated using the cameras to enforce his control, his will. It soon became something more—but I'm getting ahead of myself.

When Bruce finally moved in to his home, he moved into a white-on-white box. Not the same white on every wall or surface; in fact, it was never the same. The white on the roof was in fact more cream than white. The white on the wall in the living room was more blue than white. The white on the floor was more grey than white. The white on the bench was more yellow than white. Yes, all of these could be found on The Architect's white palette. Bruce had been asked what colors he wanted, and The Architect had listened. Then The Architect told him what he was going to get. You see, The

Architect did this with every client. He always asked them what they wanted and then told them what they would live with. He told them they could live with his decision or not. Either way. They could not change it. You see, The Architect subscribed to the "culture of the image" theory. Meaning visual stimulus eliminates the possibility of an "innocent eye." Meaning the image is always in process. Meaning each plane looks, reflects, shines, and shadows differently. And white was the perfect palette for light and shadow to play on.

Then there was the decoration The Architect let Bruce have. It was a tasty olio of high and low. Raw and cooked. Traditional and avant-garde. Flea market and design. It had Hella Jongerius fabrics and used diner furniture from dismantled steak houses. Mid-century to new modern. Ah, just looking at the cameras recording Bruce's house made me jealous and lustful. For all that Bruce had inherited.

When Bruce moved in he moved in alone. Alone. As he was four hours from the nearest living person. He moved in and followed the exact procedure The Architect had printed for him. He turned on the power grid. Opened the windows to "thirty-eight degrees." He took photos of everything and logged them on his phone so he would never forget how the house was to look. He also e-mailed it to himself as backup, just in case he lost his phone. Then, totally unscripted, Bruce took his clothes off and sat bare-assed on the flea market chair. He sat and he farted. And no one heard. No one heard him scream in delight as he farted. No one heard him. No one, except The Architect and me. And for that Bruce was to be punished. It would not be today. But it would happen when he least expected it.

On Bruce's second outing. After he had driven four hours in the hot desert sun to get to his secret "house of immense magnificence," Bruce approached his artistically corroded steel door with a cocky smile on his face. It was a smile that said, "Fuck you." It said, "Fuck you," to The Architect. It said, "Fuck you," to me. To everyone in the world. Everyone who inhabited the earth. Everyone who was not there right then. To everyone who had not heard him fart. And with that Bruce inserted the key. The fifteen cylinders sprung to life. The steel telescopic pins that were drill resistant released the door with overwhelming confidence. Everything inside Bruce's house was safe. Just where he had left it.

As Bruce pushed open the door the cocky smirk was slapped off his face. The stale, week-old air that was sealed in his home had been laced with rotting food. Bruce vomited as he walked in. Cupping his hands so he would not soil the floor, pulling his T-shirt up to his mouth, he involuntarily spewed forth the entire contents of his stomach into his shirt. He swung around as fast as he could, heading for the openness of the desert. And he vomited some more. When he stopped Bruce noticed he had vomit splatter across everything he wore. His singlet. His jeans. His shoes. So he stripped right there. He kept his socks on to stop the desert floor from burning the soles of his feet. Then Bruce looked for something to put across his face to stop the stench of death from entering his nose and mouth, making him vomit again; even if he did have nothing left in his stomach, he knew he would at least dry heave. Bruce looked around, and all he could find was a jade cactus. Luckily for Bruce it did not have spikes. Bruce tore off a leaf and pressed it under his nose. But each time he tried to hold it in with his top lip it fell. So he tore off two smaller pieces, sticking them solidly into each nostril until they were stuck fast. Bruce took deep breath after deep breath. Then held it for all he was worth.

Bruce took his first step into his house and slipped on his own vomit that had sprayed on the floor, releasing his held breath as he hit the ground and slid face first into the wall.

Bruce scrambled upright. Taking no breath. He fiddled with the windows. Opening them to ninety degrees. Can you believe it? Ninety degrees! When Bruce knew they were only ever to open to thirty-eight degrees, which formed the perfect aesthetic if you were looking at the side profile of the house The Architect designed when viewed from outside. So Bruce would also be punished for this.

Bruce ran out. Then back in. Breath held each time. Until all the windows and doors were open. Letting out the stench.

Bruce then set about putting water in a bucket and washing out every inch of his fridge. His freezer. His floor. His clothes. And while he watched everything drying, standing naked in the small patch of shade by the front door, he looked down at his penis and saw that even it was too distressed. Oh well.

Bruce checked the fuse box, restarting the main, and smiled when his fridge purred into action. He turned the air-conditioning on, and even though it was all escaping into the desert, he smiled.

Bruce's third weekend in his desert home started like the rest of them. High in expectation. Low in delivery. As Bruce inserted the key into the fifteen cylinders of protection he held his breath just in case. He rushed to the insulated windows and opened them. But it was fine. He was wrong. And pleased to be so.

Bruce set about undressing himself until he was naked. I don't know why he did this every time he entered his house, but he did, and I have the footage to verify it. Bruce stood there naked but for his socks. His old. Saggy. Floppy. Thick blue socks. Even in summer he wore heavy-grade socks. I can only imagine how they smelled, tinea and all. Bruce stood and shook himself around like a wet dog. The only difference was the lack of liquid flying. I should know—I replayed it at one thousand frames a second. And there was definitely no splash.

Just when Bruce felt his most cocky, another punishment was inflicted on him. *For what?* you ask. For the ninety-degree window opening! And with that I flicked the switch.

The minute Bruce touched anything metal based. Or metal backed. Or metal anything. Which was everything as the house was metal skinned and framed. He was electrocuted. They were small sharp shocks at first. But they built. Built in intensity and built in length. The short bursts raised the hairs on his body. Steadily increasing in strength to the point of fibrillation. Then the power supply just stopped. Bruce thought he could almost have imagined it until it started again. As he sat. As he stood. As he walked. As he swayed and grabbed the wall to hold himself up. As he swayed and pressed his limp penis against the in-built cupboards.

The shocks were now more sustained. Sustained to the point that Bruce was nearing ventricular fibrillation. The power being injected into Bruce was not enough to throw him across the room and away from the source. It was just enough to hold him there. But Bruce was lucky this time; the current did not take the path of maximum pain. His teeth hurt. His hairs were singed on his arms, back, and pubic area. And his muscles ached, as the direct voltage was not enough to cause tissue heating, which kills more people than electrical shocks. Then just when Bruce thought it was over he was zapped again. And again and again. Remembering that repeated electrical shock can lead to neuropathy, I hoped that Bruce would not fall over. Or fall with his head onto one of the metal surfaces. Meaning he would lapse into unconsciousness, like the fugitives who sat in the electric chair. So I had to be careful. Careful not to kill Bruce.

Yes, Bruce was experiencing every last jolt as punishment. Yet before he knew it he was free. Free of the voltage. Free of the metal surfaces. Free. He staggered out the door. Free to go and call the nearest electrician. Who was at least four hours away. Which he did.

The electrician came straight away when he heard Bruce was standing at guard. Naked. Outside his own desert door. The electrician put his meter to the live circuits that harbored the life-threatening levels of voltage. But nothing happened. Nothing. There was not enough current to pop a corn kernel. The electrician was not careless in his resolve. His face wore the note of concern. His body movements harbored caution. But the multi-meter, the measurer of voltage, current, and resistance, found nothing. And suddenly the electrician's mood altered. He looked at Bruce with slight disbelief. But he never really opened up and told him so, because Bruce was in fact his client. The electrician walked over to his car and placed the multi-meter in its case. Folding his gloves, and put them back in their sealable bag. The he scribbled for a while and walked over to Bruce, who was looking to explain that it had really happened. But he looked at the electrician and realized that he didn't have to. The electrician handed him his bill. Four hours travel time, times two, as it encompassed the return journey as well. It was the weekend. So Bruce also paid the weekend penalty. Bruce looked at the bottom line and his mouth fell open. Then he slowly closed it without a whimper, without a sound. All the time the electrician never did look down at Bruce's nakedness. He was never frightened or challenged by it. And that was a real sign of professionalism, I thought.

On Monday morning Bruce stood outside The Architect's office looking at his watch. Looking and hoping the second hands would suddenly move quicker. He waited until it was 8:44 when he entered. The Architect had not yet come in. But his coffee sat on his desk. Steaming. Just as he liked it. Bruce started to tell me his story. But he just as quickly stopped.

Whether he believed I was not worthy or would have no impact on his problem I don't know. He just stopped and sat down. A folder containing the specification diagrams of his house sat on his lap. It was all he could do not to fumble with the folder and get the drawings out, fingering them and pointing to the safety switches that were to be installed to stop something like this happening. But he didn't. He held himself tight. As tight as a wound-up spring.

As soon as The Architect walked into the office Bruce could hold himself no longer. He fumbled the folder, spilling the contents to the floor. The Architect walked over the diagrams; his neat little footprint now stenciled on the multi-colored images. Bruce tried to pull them from under his feet. But he could not. He could not until The Architect drank from his coffee cup, savoring the morning ritual that had become his. It was then and only then that The Architect even noticed Bruce. He noticed his scrawny body, bent over, near his feet. And with a sudden hop, The Architect had removed himself from the diagrams and examined his shoes for damage, wiping then with his handkerchief before he even heard a word Bruce spewed forth. The Architect listened and listened, sucking on his coffee while he paid attention. And after what seemed to be an immeasurably long time he spoke: "Impossible. Just not possible. I forgo sex to make certain it's not possible."

Yes, The Architect was correct. He could barely give himself enough time to eat properly, let alone spend time away from his computer that monitors the world's leading architectural sites 24/7 on everything architecture. Yes, sex, even with himself, was a distant past for The Architect. You see, The Architect actually equated projects with sex. He spent three months cultivating a partnership with a client and then three weeks bringing the project to life, nurturing it, agreeing to disagree on everything. Then it was six to twelve months until the unveiling. So it was like dating, followed by courting, followed by sex and breaking up. Except The Architect never broke up with any of his girlfriends. You see, well after each unveiling, well after the owner moved in, The Architect kept watch over his girlfriends.

It all started well before I joined. It started the time he had a week off, a holiday of sorts. Seven days away from drawing, away from designing. He suddenly found himself with nothing to do, so he started to fire up all of the cameras in every house he had built. He watched and saw how vulnerable all of his clients really were. He made notes and recorded their weaknesses. Weaknesses that would give him negotiating power should he ever need it. Which meant that Bruce was in a bad position, indeed.

The Architect went with Bruce to his house in the desert accompanied by an electrician and an electrical expert. They searched the house. Unplugged and replugged everything. They checked and rechecked the waveforms with the Elite Pro SP Recording Power Meter, which measures 144 different electrical parameters. They found everything was perfect. Everything was as it should be.

All four men stood outside Bruce's front door. Bruce stood dejected, hunched over, looking at his feet. The electrician and the electrical engineer stood chatting about their weekend exploits, small talk. While The Architect stood upright. His hands lightly clasped. He did not speak as much as breathe smoothly and evenly until he reached out and touched Bruce on the shoulder. The Architect's touch made Bruce jump a little. A jump that continued after The Architect removed his hand. It was more like a twitch. It could have been a residual effect from the electric shocks. Or it could be the first crack in Bruce's armor. Either way, the crack was there and I noted it.

CHAPTER 9.

On His Feet.

Bruce was sweating as he retold the story to the group assembled in the old chairs. But, as one of us already knew, this was just the start for Bruce. He had a long way to go and a lot to tell us, and for that he needed stamina. So Chairman Wild Bill sat Bruce down for a rest. Giving him time to catch his thoughts before he started reliving the rest of his adventure.

Looking around the room, Chairman Wild Bill looked directly into the eyes of The President of The Island. He sat, perfectly manicured, in his crease-proof suit. His perfectly shined black shoes and coiffured hair. All that was not right with his overall look was his mouth, which was turned down at the edges. Not intentionally. It was turned down due to events we will hear about. And it could never return to its former position; no, nothing could return it to its carefree place.

The President of The Island stood without being called. He walked with dignity to the front of the group, handing his PowerPoint presentation to Wild Bill. Waiting patiently for it to load before he presented, as he had done thousands of times prior, to a group waiting on his every word. The first slide loaded as he introduced himself in a staccato voice: "Welcome, gentlemen. For all of you who know me I am The President of The Island. For those whom do not, you soon will." And with that he took a deep breath, as if he was going deep sea diving for pearls.

All ears were open to hear The President of The Island's story.

The story was sincere. It was exact. It had little emotion running through it, for now. So let me explain fully to bring you up to speed. You see, The Corporate President hurt The Architect. He didn't injure him physically. He didn't insult the wife he didn't have. He didn't steal his car. Or throw garbage onto his front lawn. But he did injure his pride. He did insult his design philosophy. He did hurt his integrity. He did cut him to the quick when he showed The Architect the ultimate disrespect by buying chairs The Architect designed. But they were fakes. Fucking fakes. Can you believe it? The Architect couldn't.

And that was when I was put to the ultimate test. It's when I shone like a bright burning globe in the dead of the darkest night. I attracted all the moths to my flame. I made them dance around me. Their wings fluttering. Ready to be swatted.

As you know, The Architect had me track down every winning contractor who tendered to work on The Corporate President's new building, The Island. Every bolt maker. Every lumber supplier. Every plumbing contractor. Every electrical wiring guy. Every brick supplier. Every concrete truck owner. Every steel fixer. Every forger. Every roofer. Every importer. Every building broker. Every tap maker. Glass fixer. Tiler. Grout supplier. Landscape designer. Gardener. Everyone that was anyone on The Corporate President's job was in my Filofax. And that's when The Architect drew up his finest plan. Like a swarm of hummingbirds filling the blank page until all that remained was a plan so perfect The Corporate President of The Island would feel the wrath of The Architect for many months to come. I will let The Corporate President tell it in his own words.

The Corporate President looked a little nervous out front of the group. I bet it was the first time in an age, the first time since he was a Yale upstart giving a presentation in a cheap suit, his shoes over-shiny, his tie the wrong color, his belt not matched to his shoes. The first feeling of insecurity since way back then. It must have been a feeling he had long forgotten. But today it was back, and it was taking over his normally pristine social mannerisms. His voice stammered, slightly at first. It stammered and then faltered. His voice box lost its normal deep tone and scratched and broke and froze. His lips and tongue looked dry. He swallowed more often than not after each word. He looked like he was swallowing dry birdseed. His words seemed to spit out the seeds in the direction of the group. I moved my hand to cover my face, but nothing fell on me. It must have been an illusion. But The President of The Island felt it. His words squeaked out as single notes. Until the single notes joined up to make words. Then sentences. Then his story. And what a story it was.

"The Architect was approached by me initially to design the multimillion-dollar headquarters for my corporation, for The Island Headquarter Project. We called it The Island because it was like we had our little Barbados. Our own

Naples. Our own deserted island surrounded by water. Our own oasis.

"But The Architect refused. Over nothing, really. Well, it was over something. Over the fact that we bought replicas of his single chair. I did not know that they were replicas until after he examined them, called me a cunt, and walked out."

The group gasped when he said the *cunt* word. But our reactions did not rattle him, not one bit. The President was getting into his rhythm. His face was starting to color up. Yes, he was at last in his stride.

"Once The Architect walked away I thought I had seen the last of him. Well, I had, in a way. I didn't see him again for a long while. But he was obviously looking at me, from afar, behind the cloaks of others."

It was just then that The President forgot the logical order of his story and came to the end with such ferocity that he nearly split his mouth with the venom that frothed forth from it.

"I remember the first time it happened. It must have been at least one month after the whole company moved to The Island. I was feeling a little cocky, a little lucky almost to have The Island as my home. That was until I opened my office door. The stench of it made me sick. I vomited all over my Grieves & Hawkes Suit."

That suit cost him fifteen thousand dollars.

"It sprayed onto my shoes and the Iranian embroidered carpet."

Iranian embroidered carpets were traditionally made by royal and aristocratic women in the home. But with the advent of commercial manufacture, primarily the introduction of steel needles and improved linen weaving, Iranian carpets became more available. Mary Stewart, Queen of Scots, is known to have been an avid fan of Iranian carpets and also an avid embroiderer.

"I did not know what had happened in my office. Well, not that day. But I soon found out that it was infested. Infested with shit. Piss. Sperm. It was as if an orgy had happened in my office. On my sofa. On my floor. Then everyone at the orgy had pissed and shitted after they fucked. My office was a brothel. I had the cleaning company come in and sanitize the whole room. The carpet was totally replaced that day. As were the lounges. The chairs. The sofa. Everything. And by the time I left work at 8:00 p.m. everything was as it should be. Until the next morning.

"I remember opening the door the next day and finding that the stench was the same. I gagged and managed to hold back the urge to vomit. I took a deep breath and had a look around. The orgy had happened again. The fucking. The shitting. The soiling. And it happened again the next day. And the next. And the next. And the next. I had The Corporation set up cameras in my office to document who was having an orgy. And the next day I viewed the footage. At exactly 1:00 a.m. there was suddenly a surge of water rats. I had no idea how they got in, but they overtook my space. They chewed on my expensive chairs. They fucked on my rug and shat on my carpet. They rolled over and over in their own feces and scratched and pissed everywhere. It was as if my island was infested. And at exactly 5:00 a.m. they were gone. All that was left was their aftermath. It seemed the water rats came in from a hatch in the floor inside my private bathroom, directly above the water of The Island, through a pipe that connected the outside to the inside. So I had exterminators take over my office. They sat in shifts whenever I vacated. They sat there, cages at the ready. But the water rats did not return. Day after day they waited. Nothing.

"I felt at ease again working on The Island in my impressive office. I felt great smelling the fresh leather of my new chairs. The smell of the new Iranian carpet. The smell of my freshly sanitized room. Then, one morning, it must have been exactly one month since the exterminators left The Island empty-handed, I opened my office and saw that the destruction had begun again. This time the water rats were ravenous. Hungry. Destructive. And full of shit. Because there was shit everywhere. Splattered. It had splattered up the walls. On my mahogany desk. On my leather desk mat. On my Aurora Diamante pen."

The pen is topped with a diamond cabochon—a polished, not faceted gem that was further decorated with almost two thousand De Beers 4C gems on a solid platinum barrel ... I could imagine the water rats rubbing the pen between their legs while the other rats fucked them, but that's just me.

"On the chewed leather chairs. The soiled Ostrich leather fabric sofa."

Ostrich is one of the most precious natural leathers in the world with a tensile strength of three to five times that of cowhide. Over time it would have become more soft, delicate, and bright. Ostrich contains natural oils that resist hardening and drying and remains soft and firm. The uniqueness is the naturally forming bumps ... if only The President's ostrich leather could speak.

"And all across the carpet. My Iranian carpet. And then it was front page in the press. Photos. Documented evidence. So I had my legal team subpoena the exterminators. The cleaners. The carpet company. The furniture emporium. Everyone was slapped with a do-not-speak clause. But the evidence did not stop. It fed the newspapers like ink on a page. It ran and made thick black passages of type that howled from the rooftops that The Island was flawed. Faulty. Ill-conceived. A waste of shareholders' money. A folly."

Okay, it's time I took over. The President's picture is not the full one. It's his side of the story. Now you will hear the true side, the calculated side—the Architect's side.

You know, The Architect had me find every manufacturer of every supplier of product that would go into The Island. Well, I found my specialty supplier in the Pipe Man. There were literally hundreds of kilometers of pipes of every description for every convenience. Heating. Ventilation. Air-conditioning. Managing thermal comfort. Indoor air quality. Filtration. Maintaining of pressure relationships between spaces. Every pipe was designed, analyzed, and purpose purpose-built by building engineers. Pipes lay on pipes. Over pipes. Making tunnels that ran the height of the building. Ran, the length of the floor, sometimes several times. Twisting like a snake. Showing their outside form. While hiding what's inside. It was the perfect protection.

The colors of the pipes sat on top of one another like a rainbow, like several rainbows. Inside the pipes could live billions of ants. Millions of small mice. Or a colony of rats. The pipe coatings were impenetrable, making them resistant to animals and humans alike. The pipes had seals that were rubber gaskets. Gaskets of the compression type. There were pipes that were fuel-resistant. Pipes that discharged massive quantities of water at elevated temperatures. Pipes that handled septicity. Sanitary sewer systems. Gravity flow lines. Covers. Appurtenances. Ductile iron castings. Catch basins. Thermoplastic.

Basically the pipes were in place to take the shit away from the thousand dollar units someone just shat in. Yep, it was a vital design of any building. A design that if it failed would flood your house or your office, with your own excrement. Yep, shit. Toilet paper. Water. Piss.

I managed to source every one of the shit merchants before they came on site. They hated being called shit merchants, but that's what they were. As highly paid as doctors that look up your ass. The only difference is that these shit merchants occasionally had to get their hands dirty.

Yes, I documented everything and had fun doing it. I documented the sexiness of the shit pipes as they lay across and around all the other pipes. I documented the flow, the fall, the volume, the patterns and roads they created. These were roads no one would ever see or appreciate unless you were the shit merchants or the electrical engineers or the IT tech heads. Or me.

Yes, I got to see them before they were built, during their build, and post-build. I got to trace each and every pipe from the get-go to its delivery point. And that's how the rats got in.

In fact these pipes were a lot like our own bodies. Just looking at the pipes the first time I was suddenly excited. The kind of excitement experienced when the erogenous zones become gorged with blood. When we become excited. Sending signals. Suppressing signals. Building the fluid of creation and spurting it out into the bloodstream of a building, or a body. That building of fluid was happening in my own body, as it was being mimicked in the very pipes I was lusting over.

The pipes were impregnating the mother ship. The mother ship being The Island. Impregnating it with power to burn the lights bright. Impregnating it with water to cleanse, with enough volume to flush away the feces and rubbish.

The impregnation was evident on every floor. At every desk. At every power outlet. At every computer. The impregnation was evident above and below those in the office, and all the while those in the office took it for granted. But not me. I was in awe as the heated floors gave warmth. As the walls soaked up sound, sucking it in and nullifying it like a giant balloon that swallowed screams. As the ceilings covered and protected those below. As the vents warmed the air, keeping it at the perfect temperature for optimum personal performance, sending out quiet songs of confidence and calm. Yes, the pipes below, which were the skeleton of The Island, were to me like the nervous system of the body, running miles and miles, laying above and below the veins of office life. Yet all the time hidden by the façade of the building, protecting the sex of the pipes. Just like the leather jacket currently pulled over my shoulder hiding my bony torso. Or my jeans hiding my sex. Or your skirt hiding yours.

If only everyone could see the inside of The Island as I did. It was as if I were the gynecologist inspecting the building's pregnant womb. Full of growing life. Full of growing expectation. And only in time would the building's true potential be born.

See, The Architect unknowingly gave me the project of the century. A project I would never have experienced had he not wanted revenge. The President of The Island was correct: revenge happened at exactly the same time each night—1:00 a.m., when a group of sewer rats was enticed with food into the shit pipes.

The shit merchants had installed an electric door that cut off the flow of water and shit and let the rats directly into The President's office. They crawled up through the toilet bowl itself into his elite bathroom, across the hideously expensive tiles, and out into the office. So they could root and shit and spoil the place for hours before being lured away at exactly 5:00 a.m. out the same way they came. Undetected. Unnoticed. Until the morning.

It was my job to make it happen, and I did. I watched it via another miniscule camera. I watched it and recorded the mayhem. I replayed it with glee. I tried to show it to The Architect, but he wasn't interested. He was only interested that it had happened, and he seemed to lose interest the instant it had. But not me. I watched it night after night. I put a stop to it once the pest controllers took occupancy of the office at night. But it surprised them when I had the rats come back when they thought it was all over. Ha. But that was just the start. The papers miraculously got hold of the story, the photographs, and the footage. The President of The Island was in for a lot more than he ever expected.

Chapter 10.

The Architect Growing Up.

I think it's time I gave you some background on The Architect and his home life growing up.

You see, both his mother and his father molded his career. They were prosthetic technicians. Sculptors. Perfectionists. But not your normal sculptors. The Architect's mother and father sculpted for special victims. Victims of war. Violence. Hatred. Ethnicity. They sculpted prosthetic breasts. Penises. Ball bags, and butt cheeks.

The Architect grew up with naked people in his parent's studio. They worked all the time. He was an only child. They had no backyard, so he played happily among the false breasts and penises, among the bums and single butt cheeks. He learned to mold from real-life models. White penises. Black penises. Circumcised and uncircumcised. Flaccid and erect.

When he was helping out, taking molds of the erect

penises, if they became flaccid he would call in his mother, who could do wonders with a flaccid penis. And before he knew it, it was erect. Yes, The Architect knew from an early age what race had the biggest penis. What race was mostly circumcised. Yes, he mostly knew about male body parts, except for the occasional woman who needed a replacement breast. You see, The Architect never saw a naked woman's vagina until he was in college. But what he did know was the correct texture a man's penis should have, the correct ribbing, the correct veins, the crevices. He told me that in a strange way it taught The Architect to appreciate his profession. Architecture. It taught him about form. Line. Shape. Curves. Length. Volume. It taught him to design a building to stand out or to remain hidden until all was revealed on closer inspection.

It also taught him that there was a market outside his parents' relatively small business providing body parts for returned servicemen and women. The ones whose ass had been blown off by a bomb or had their penis fall off due to foreign hookers or their tits savaged by disease. He knew there was a broader market. How he knew this I was not sure. However, one day he woke and decided to start a sex toy business of his own.

His parents were pleased. They knew so much about dicks and asses and tits, so they threw their workshop and knowledge right behind The Architect. They became his co-designers. Co-designers of tight-fitting butt plugs. Co-designers, of life-like dildos. And for the very first time the toys were in different colors. Not just black and white. They were coffee colored like the Mexicans, yellow like the Asians, red like the native Indians and the Indians from the Amazon, green like the color of live seaweed, purple like his mother's favorite scarf, orange like the grove, silver like the weather balloons. You see, The Architect and his parents hit on a gold mine when they turned the unknown into the known. And it all went very well, indeed.

Momma even became an inventor of her own when she made a prototype of a female vibrator. She even tested it on herself. The Architect was never sure how she came up with the idea or the notion, but it was a revelation. Momma's model was based on a small metal arm attached to an old fashioned sewing machine that she foot-operated as she sat, legs open, with one of the big molded rubber penises attached to it. It did the job as her random late-night cries certified as they echoed from the workshop while The Architect's father lay fast asleep, an empty bottle of liquid sleeping pills sitting nearby. It seemed like the perfect household to The Architect. And who was I to question him.

What I do know for sure is that the money he made from his sex toy business paid for his parent's house, put The Architect through school and college, and paid for his degree. And even now it let him pick and choose the projects he wanted to take on as The Architect.

Money was no longer his major concern. But it was a great concern that he charge his clients the right amount for his excellence. And for that excellence they would pay dearly.

The night The Architect told me all this, he must have been a little intoxicated, drunk with the secrets he had never told anyone. He told me through a clenched fist, through clenched teeth. He told me and me alone that he kept the last samples of strap-on penises and balls, of asses in different shapes, of breasts large and small, the last samples his parents ever made, in a locked box in his wardrobe, in his home. He kept them after his parents died. Tragically.

How did his parents die, you ask? I do not recount the story flippantly. It seemed the sewing machine went berserk. It was a power surge after the flood. The electrical system in his parents' home was having trouble conducting electricity evenly. His parents were advised to hire an electrician as the sudden surges could cause a fire or fry the internal appliances if the surge travelled at the speed of light through damaged wires. Which is just what the police think happened.

It was late at night. Momma was using the sewing machine, but not for sewing. She had her favorite gold metal penis attached to it. The weather had been foul. Pappa was drunk. Asleep. The Architect was away. And Momma had some sewing of her own to do. The electrical surge ran through the wires like a case of syphilis through an army squadron. It ran through the sewing machine, through the metal arm, and through the gold penis as it burned every inch of hair from his mother's vagina. And when The Architect's father woke to her screaming he ran downstairs and grabbed her, trying to pull her free from the spinning molded penis. Alas, he too was fried. They were fried until the sewing machine could no longer handle it and fused the entire building into darkness.

If that wasn't painful enough, The Architect was the one to make the grisly find. He had been away on a study trip for a full week. When he returned, under the eye of a torch, he found his poor parents. He screamed and broke down in tears that nearly flooded his home. His world as he knew it was gone forever. His parents had taught him what a naked man and woman looked like, but the sight of his mother and her sewing was too much. He ran from the room. Screaming. Waking his neighbor, Mrs. Smitz. Who covered his parents to save dignity.

The Architect was the first human to find his parents; however, he told me through wet nose and ruddy cheeks that they were found by something way before him. Rats had found them and had been feasting on his mother's wide-open legs. It was something he told me he would never forget. Rats became his phobia. His sign for ultimate destruction.

The authorities put it down to a sex game gone wrong. Hence the case was closed. There was no report in the newspaper. No indignity to defend.

The Architect, Mrs. Smitz and the people who modeled for the moldings all attended the funeral. The Architect spoke with emotion. With tears. He spoke of his loving parents. They were his world, and now they were gone. In their honor The Architect stopped the output of his sex toy business for one whole month.

Sadly it had become the responsibility of The Architect to dismantle the sewing machine and its attachments. He kept them. The sewing machine. The metal arm. The gold penis. He kept them alongside his parents' moldings. He kept them hidden. Hidden away in his wardrobe.

Hearing this story after hours in the closed office was the most intimate I had been with The Architect. I remember it so clearly. He told me he would never forgive electricity or rats.

He then confided in me about his time away at college straight after his parent's death. He went to live on campus as he could no longer stand the memory of burned flesh that could not be flushed out of his parents' home.

The Architect found out lots about mankind at college. People who would do anything to win over a girl, or a friend, or a jock. People who would do anything including fucking over their friends to be accepted. And that's just what happened to The Architect. He foolishly told a close friend and roommate that he made models of body parts. And that's when it started. The guys on the football team wanted to show off manhood they did not have. And so the orders for flaccid penis pouches began. A penis pouch was a slightly oversized penis and ball bag combination. It was tied to the body with an invisible group of straps, making the wearer look like he had a big, natural package. The jocks made appointments to have their own penis pouches made to measure. But that was not what hurt him. What hurt The Architect was his roommate, the one who introduced him to Mia. Yes, her name was Mia—his first girlfriend at college. She was pretty in a horsey kind of way. Her hair was—yes you guessed it—more like a flowing main than the coiffured look. But she was his. He didn't dare to show her off in fear that someone would steal her. So he met her at night. They held hands in the dark. In the shadows of the college. They met until they were a real item. Until it had become time for more than a kiss. The Architect knew what was next.

He had witnessed many erect penises and knew what they were to look like. In anticipation he inspected his own penis and found that it looked nothing like his expectations. So he delayed the inevitable as long as he could. He examined his penis in the mirror nightly. He poked it and pulled it; prodded it and stroked it. He tried to get it to resemble the erections in his parents' home. Yet even after all he had witnessed, he did look in amazement once his own thick blue vein ran the length of it. But he quickly realized several inadequacies. The head of his penis was not proud enough. His shaft was not thick enough. His size was not sizeable enough. And he knew that a true man, like the ones in his parent's workshop, could maintain an erect penis for the fifteen minutes it took to take a mold. After playing with his own penis, The Architect discovered that his only ever stayed erect for a few minutes at best.

When Mia and The Architect were finally alone he knew what to do. He had been told hundreds of times by the men in his parents workshop. They told him stories of their conquests while they stood still. And erect.

But The Architect still got caught, in an admiring kind of

way. You see, when Mia took her top and bra off The Architect was transfixed by the beauty and form of her breasts. Her perfectly placed nipples. The fall to the side of her volume. He studied them like a doctor when he should have been stroking them and sucking them. But Mia forgave him. After all she had heard about his exploits on campus and could not wait to see what penis pouch The Architect had. And that's where it all went wrong. The Architect slid under the bed covers and took off his underwear apprehensively, while Mia threw back the blankets and demanded to see his penis pouch. The Architect explained that his was an average package, moving his hands away to expose it. Mia looked and laughed. She laughed so hard The Architect's semi-erect penis deflated. It deflated to such an extent that it almost became inverted. It became soft and shy and cold and white. Not red and full of blood. Not rock hard and bursting with sperm. It became, in Mia's words, "a very poor excuse for a penis." So poor in fact that she suggested that The Architect wear a penis pouch during sex. And that's when The Architect snapped. It was as if a sexual monster suddenly took over his body. He snapped and said, well if that was what Mia wanted then she could sit (actually sit) on this, and he produced a magnificently made eight-inch, thick black jelly cock. In fact a dildo. His black-market special. And with that Mia was again in love with The Architect. She begged him to beat her with it. And he consented. He beat her softly about her wet mouth, slapping her bright red lips with it. Then he slapped her pert nipples and perfectly shaped breasts with it. Then her pelvic bone, which stuck out and made an obvious target for a slapping. Then he teased her as he slapped it around her vagina, as she begged him to insert it. But he did not. He could not. It was supposed to be his own penis that Mia should have begged for. But she begged for the black-market special, so he stopped right there. She begged for it while he flopped there, flaccid and indignant. Mia stormed out of his room, leaving him alone with his small penis.

The next day the whole college knew about his exploits. They laughed at him openly. Openly. About his small penis. His small, flaccid, cold, white penis. Yet, that very same day, he was inundated with orders from the girls at college for a version of the black-market special. And he agreed. Agreed to supply them so he could guarantee his future. He apologized in prayers to his dead mother and father, as he was again in full production.

I listened to the story with a tear. And I watched him closely. Almost microscopically. I watched and recorded every swish of his fingers against his hair. Every slight grimace. Every turn up of his mouth. Every flare of his nostrils. I remember him sitting there thinking about the past events that had molded his life. And right out of the blue. Like a rifle shot that startled the world. Like a John F. Kennedy shot. He coined the phrase: "You know, great buildings are the tits and ass of the skyline. Everyone wants their piece of them. Everyone wants to touch them. Everyone wants to see a little more of them."

And if I didn't know before this, I knew it then. The Architect was like no other architect in the world!

Chapter 11.

Till Death Do Us Part.

Wild Bill stepped up to The President and put a hand on his shoulder. Reassuring him. Showing understanding. Wild Bill lowered his head, and the two grown men walked to his ugly chair where The President of The Island lowered himself into the over-bulbous fabric that seemed to swallow him. Hiding him from himself and his tales of The Architect. His tales of the rats and the public disgrace.

Wild Bill stood before the group again. This time it was his story we were going to hear. Like a preacher reaching out to his flock his words were full of passion.

"The Architect told me marriage was like a building. It had solid foundations. It had love. It created kinship. It highlighted interpersonal relationships. It was intimate. Sexy. It was the union of shape and form. It encompassed the legal, economic, spiritual, and even religious. And it housed the nuclear family unit."

Wow. Beautifully put. Because Wild Bill's building was just like that. His building was his home. His home was recognized by the state and architectural community as a brilliant piece of design. His legal obligation was to look after it. Nurture it. Love it, and hopefully appreciate it until the day he died. The building, that is. And to do nothing The Architect wouldn't approve of.

We all knew that Wild Bill had signed his life away when he decided to have The Architect build his second home. It was his marriage to The Architect. It was their union that was founded and agreed upon. Not based on love. But based on the prenuptial that The Architect would pour all of his soul into a home he would never own himself. Wild Bill was the receiver of such a gift. He would pay The Architect handsomely. And never. Ever. Change one thing.

That respect was a professional pact both parties would honor like a marriage.

When it came to his wife Trophy, there was no such legal obligation for Wild Bill. No prenuptial. There was, however, a manly obligation, because Wild Bill's wife was another matter altogether. She may be wife number two, but even though she did not know it, she was every bit as showy as his house—I stand corrected: as their house. She was the only one for Wild Bill, and hopefully that would stay that way until the day she died. Or Wild Bill killed her.

Yes, Wild Bill's house was original. Beautiful. And camera-laden. It just happened that most of the hidden cameras in Wild Bill's house were placed in the eagle's nest—the bedroom. There was nowhere to hide. But it didn't matter to Wild Bill. He had no reason to doubt his wife. So he presumed that there was no reason to see any of the tapes, any of the performances from the eagle's nest.

He had agreed to every piece of footage being documented and scrutinized and then eventually disregarded. He knew that all the footage was held for three months and then erased if Wild Bill did not ask to see it. He knew that someone was watching the footage. What he didn't know was that The Architect also viewed the images after me daily. And I always erased them, until one night.

The night in question, Wild Bill was more than a little drunk. He and his Trophy wife had been out to a design forum. The discussion topic was "What Makes a Livable City?" There were hundreds of architectural answers to the all-important question. It was all about sustainability. It focused on urban planners, investors, politicians, and most importantly, people. People with an inspired view of design. The forum was not to instantly solve the world's problems. Rather, it was about impressing the point that design, good design, great design, could help. It was about design taking up the challenge and redeveloping systems that propel individuals, society, and business into the future.

Wild Bill heard all they had to say. But he was not really interested. It didn't affect him, holed up in his cocoon. It didn't affect his wife. Or their life. It was all about showing up. All about pressing the flesh. All about making sure everyone knew he was the owner of The Architect's house.

Wild Bill was so elated to be recognized by the design crowd that he drank too much of the free champagne. He drove home too fast. He popped a Viagra tablet just before he entered his car. He asked his Trophy to blow him during the drive, but she refused. She peppered him with promises from the eagle's nest instead. She even mentioned The Architect and how lucky they were to know him.

Wrong thing to do. Wrong. Wrong. Wrong.

Wild Bill misconstrued her comment for a possible ménage a trois. A fantasy. And he was furious. Furious that his Trophy would—could—even think that The Architect could possibly match him in bed. That The Architect could possibly join in their sex life. Unless of course he was being fucked by Wild Bill while Trophy watched. Documenting it with pictures, so Wild Bill could blackmail The Architect whenever he wanted. Meaning he could change things in his house at random without repercussion.

Entering the eagle's nest, the very thought of The Architect threw Wild Bill into a rage. All his blood went straight to his head when in fact he wanted it to go straight to his penis. You see, Viagra only works when the man is stimulated. I think it's time for a small medical lesson. A lesson Wild Bill should have learned!

Normally body parts are moved using muscles. But not your penis. It is completely different. No muscle contractions are involved in making your penis erect. Instead, the penis uses pressure. The easiest way to explain how the penis becomes erect is to think of it as a balloon. No air, no balloon. Inflate the balloon and it becomes elongated. Add more and more air and it becomes rigid. But that's not the reason Wild Bill asked his wife to "blow him." No. Wild Bill wanted Trophy to suck his penis to pressurize it. So it would blow up like a balloon. To allow the blood to flow rapidly into it. The pressurized blood trapped. The penis erect. Hard. Ready.

Recovering from his head spin. Calming himself, and thinking of what he was about to give up, Wild Bill took time to use the right words. He also took charge and ordered, nicely, that Trophy keep the promise that she made in the car. And she did. She was happy to get it over and done with and relieve the stress Wild Bill was feeling by pressurizing his penis. But the session was not going to be a short one. The alcohol Wild Bill had consumed stopped his normal sensitive feelings connecting with his blood-enriched penis, and his ability to come was compromised. Compromised to the point where Wild Bill had plenty of time to insult The Architect during the sex session, which he did. He also forgot the promise to himself to be nice to Trophy and reap the rewards.

Wild Bill started off his insulting rant as he made love to his wife. Would you call it love? He had his penis firmly stuck in his Trophy's throat as he asked her unanswerable questions.

"Do you think The Architect could fill your throat like this? Well, do you? Do you?" At this point he totally lost it and started screaming and yelling. I won't go into too much detail albeit to say that he flipped her over and over and used his blood-enriched penis as a weapon. A weapon of disrespect. To his Trophy and to The Architect.

When his brain and his penis finally connected almost forty-five minutes had gone. He fell onto the bed beside Trophy and immediately realized what he had done. Yet his response was slowed and groggy.

Trophy's response was immediate. It was cold. The complete opposite of the doll-like object he had thrown around. The opposite of the warm-blooded vessel he had occupied for the past forty-five minutes. Her response was swift. He responded like the beast of a jock he was and pleaded with her to forgive him. He begged. He offered presents. Money. Then he cried. He cried for her forgiveness. For her understanding.

Trophy stopped on her way to the stunning en suite bathroom. She looked back at him confidently as she told him, "Right now I wish it had been The Architect that just fucked me." And with that she turned on the shower to wash away the smell of Wild Bill.

Wild Bill stopped. Frozen. Until he had time to digest what had just been spat at him. He threw open the shower door. The mist from the hot water smudged the camera in the ceiling and the one between the showerhead and the taps on the wall just enough to blur the footage marginally. But not enough to stop The Architect from hearing Wild Bill say "that little cunt wouldn't have enough cock in his pants to take a piss, let alone fuck a Trophy. That little cunt would come just at the sight of your tits. Let alone your pussy. That little cunt has probably never had a fuck in his life. That little cunt doesn't have the force to take you. Doesn't have the masculinity. Doesn't have the physical power. Doesn't have the shoulders. The broad chin. The high cheekbones." Wild Bill flexed his toned body, watching himself in the mirror. And with that the shower door was closed in his face.

Wild Bill had to temper his want to open it and smash his Trophy in the face. But he had learned his lesson. He had done that to his first wife, and no good came from it. So he hurled the last abuse before he dressed and drove to the nearest strip joint.

"Maybe you should call that little cunt and arrange to go shopping next time you need to buy sanitary pads. I'm sure he knows where the best place to shop is. Where you can pay ten times more for a pack wrapped in twenty-four-carat gold foil." And with that he was gone.

Wild Bill's Trophy stood in the shower for what seemed like an hour, washing and rewashing herself. Rinsing and re-rinsing her mouth with mouth wash. She was upset. But not to the point of leaving him.

There was no such luck with The Architect. He was going to divorce Wild Bill once he saw the tape. Once I showed him, in the room where I watched the tape, The Architect's secret room that recorded each and every camera from each and every house he ever built. It had charts documenting of all the owners' blueprints of all the designs. Photos of every room. Every cornice. Every tap handle. Every floor covering. It had score sheets, and the individual owners were marked as occupants, scored from one to ten. I was just about to find out that he also judged them as people. Good. Bad. Honest. Dishonest. Weak. Nice. Deserving. Punishable. He had a formula. You see, every Sunday evening as if he was going to the movies The Architect showered. Dressed. Bought popcorn from the office kitchen, and sat with earphones on to view the weekly events of his occupants. The viewing room was more like a high-tech home theater. But there was just one chair. Multiple screens. And one master controller.

The Architect always started with his newest house, the one where the owners, even second timers, might have ideas of their own. Where the owners who might think they have the right to change something in their own home without asking The Architect. When he started to view Wild Bill's home he put up the transparent drawings of his home and viewed them against the real projections for every room in the home to make sure there was status quo. Which there was. It was just the action going on in the eagle's nest that I insisted he see. Action that garnered his attention.

The Architect had not had sex with a woman, or a man, since before the problem on campus with his then-girlfriend Mia. It had had such a massive impact on him that he used his celibacy to channel every inch of his energy into great design. He had done it for so long that he doubted his own ability to design without being celibate. But I will go into that later. Tonight The Architect was aroused by the fast-forward action between Wild Bill and his Trophy. Don't get me wrong. The Architect had fast-forwarded their sex action many, many times before. But for some reason tonight, thanks to my prodding, he slowed it down and enjoyed himself while he munched his popcorn.

I had paused the action from the minute Wild Bill and Trophy entered the eagle's nest. I had the volume raised so he could hear their banter. The Architect scoffed to himself at Wild Bill's slight drunk stammer, at his self-worth. But he changed his view when he saw Wild Bill's fully erect penis. It was a beauty. A specimen. As good as he could remember. Even compared to the big black models he molded in his parents' workshop. It stood like a skyscraper. An arrow into the clouds. A colossus. The Architect was mesmerized by it. Until he saw Trophy. Until I turned the volume all the way up to drown out the vision. And that's when he heard Wild Bill's rant. His personal attack on The Architect.

The Architect listened and rewound it and listened again. Just to make sure he was not imagining it. After the third run-through The Architect paused the replay and looked down at the scribbling on the freehand notepad he used to scribble house plans he had involuntarily made. The same word was written over and over again: Mia. Mia. Mia.

CHAPTER 12.

The Puppet Master.

The shock he felt viewing the footage from the eagle's nest put The Architect on edge. If Wild Bill was defaming him what were the others saying? And with that The Architect became a true detective of his homes. He scoured every inch of every tape. He saw Bruce tentatively walk around his desert palace, wincing at every touch of an appliance. Wincing as he turned the shower on. Wincing as he turned his satellite LCD screen on. Wincing as he sat down. The Architect made a note to call and visit Bruce just to set him straight and stop his wincing.

The Architect watched The President of The Island on the single camera in an early edition of his New Modern Discovery House. Yes, The President owned one of The Architect's homes. That was how he knew to contact him for The Island project. The only problem with The President and his early edition of The Architect's design was that there was just one camera installed, originally mounted high in the bedroom wall to catch out a philandering wife. And now all it did was occasionally shine down on the shiny silver hair of The President of The Island as he placed his face on the pronounced breasts of his equal-aged wife. Something told The Architect that she had had work.

The rest of his houses featured 108 cameras in total. And they were all examined. Examined and studied. It took over The Architect. It became his priority. An hour could not go by without The Architect walking past a camera recording and rewinding the action.

Each camera had a motion sensor, which The Architect turned on at my insistence. And once he had gone through all the archival footage to save his reputation, he reacted personally to each and every sensor when they were triggered. They were triggered by dogs. Children. Drunk husbands. Sexy wives. They were triggered regularly. On hearing each sensor alarm The Architect responded by getting up and watching. Rewinding, and playing back, just to make sure his name and reputation was not being vilified. He seemed to forget about his practice momentarily. Until the "r" word suddenly hit him. Revenge. Yes, revenge. A seven-letter word he had never imagined himself using once he left college. Let alone thinking about it day and night. Night and day.

It hit him like a sledgehammer. Like a bolt of lightning. Like the first thought of a great design. It hit him like a first drawing on site. The first scribble. The first pen line. It hit him, and it would hurt Wild Bill where he least expected it. It was his one potential weakness. Yes, weakness. Not The Architect's but Wild Bill's. Who, I might add, did not seem to have one. Well, not that I had imagined.

The Architect gave me specific instructions when I came to see him. It was like a blueprint. Each and every line was drawn like the hummingbird. Each and every line fed the project as a whole, like a slice of bread building a loaf. Each and every event had to take place in precise order to make the blueprint work.

The first piece to the puzzle was art. Wild Bill loved art. He loved abstract. I remember the very first painting The Architect suggested Wild Bill buy. It was a huge piece, a monstrous piece, too big for most homes. The room to house such a piece needed to be mighty substantial, and that's what Wild Bill had. It was five meters by eight meters.

The piece was sensitive. It was adventurous. Too adventurous for most, but not for Wild Bill. And it had a price tag to match: $450,000. I can see it now as if it has been ingrained into my memory. It was a monstrous white swipe of paint over a dense black background. The Architect told me that he remembered introducing Wild Bill to his gallery friend who had an art history background, and all he had to say about the painting to Wild Bill was that "this is incredibly livable." And with that Wild Bill nearly shit himself right there and then in his thousand dollar trousers. This incredibly considered opinion of the gallery owner opened Wild Bill to a new awareness of modern art. Livable it was. And livable it was to become. From that day forth Wild Bill forgot about matching art to his sofa. To his carpet. His curtains. From that day forth Wild Bill used the livable description to its maximum potential. Wild Bill said it so many times in so many correct places that it became part of the art vernacular. Livable. Extremely livable. Unbelievably livable. Which basically meant that the artist had eliminated all recognizable imagery. A copout, you say? No. The artist in question spoke of transformation, of painting into an existential drama. Not of a painting or of an event. When asked, the artist in question said he just painted it. Put paint to canvas without judgment. That's it. His gesture on canvas was a gesture of liberation. The artist also abandoned any title so he would not cloud the painting with any preconceived ideas.

This approach. This style of abstract. Of action painting. Of abstract expressionism, was not new. No. It started somewhere around the German expressionists and their combination of intensity and self-denial, with their anti-figurative aesthetic. From the abstract schools of futurism, bauhaus, and synthetic cubism. The style was widespread from the early 1940s until the early 1960s. A lot of it involved powerful black-and-white paintings using gesture. Surface. Symbol. Powerful emotional charges. Abstract landscape. Expressionistic visions of figures. You can research it; Wild Bill did. He dipped himself in it. Drenched himself in its unaffordability. In its wankery. You see, art and design, architectural design, as a sub-culture for the very rich was totally classist, and that's the way Wild Bill liked it. Yes, Wild Bill wanted it to be no more accessible to you than to me. Wild Bill wanted what every art wanker in the world wanted. Art affordable by the few.

It meant that the next big art purchase of Wild Bill's was a six meter by six meter shaved vagina. Well, that's what he said it was. All The Architect and I could see was a Grand Canyon–like crevice with a few stray, black, short trees by the side of the opening.

Then there was the dead horse. Or so Wild Bill said. I could just make out the bullet hole in a skull-like vessel, the reddish pool running down the flattened hair of a massive forequarter and leg. Wild Bill was in heaven. He became every art auctioneer's best friend. Their go-to guy when bidding stalled. Their home run when the subject matter became almost abhorrent.

The Architect knew that and planned a gallery opening of his own. And the name of the gallery was to be Revenge.

Revenge to most of us means the concept of inflicting punishment in return for injury or insult. To take vengeance. To retaliate. To inflict equal damage for the injury received. But what could equal the hurt The Architect had received at the length of Wild Bill's tongue?

Revenge in The Architect's heart meant wild justice (I added the wild part). The Architect did not care that revenge may be like biting a dog because the dog bit you. He was prepared. His revenge was to be personal. Societal. Affecting not just Wild Bill but also those attached to him. Yes, The Architect was going to get his own back and more. It was not just about getting even. It *was* about getting even. And The Architect would wait to taste the sweetness. His desire to do harm was that strong.

And so I had my work cut out, to set up the gallery "Revenge." It was not the kind of work I was used to. But I loved it. I ate it up. I seemed to shine in the deep dark depths of murkiness. My first step was to find and document "every almost-made-it artist." Abstract artists. Good-looking abstract artists. Artists who would do anything to pocket enough money to enable them to paint for a year. And there were plenty of candidates.

I documented their works. I visited them and documented via video their human characteristics. Their body shape. Their ability to have a conversation, mostly just about art. To check their art history knowledge. Their flamboyance. And their miserable ability to take the money offered for the dirty task. A man reverting to animal.

I saw in these candidates animals that had become men and could just as easily go back to being animals.

Humans are unique, you know. Via a strange event in our animal past we as humans somehow acquired culture. Evolutionists refer to it as a "critical point" in leaving the ground on all fours and speaking. We learned language. We learned to speak, which in itself is the lifeblood of culture. Language is the most momentous product of the human mind. It surpasses the animal call of love, of warning of danger. It also brings with it the disease of choice, of ability. The disease enabling man to spoil our own instincts, our own enjoyment of life. Animals, predators, hunt without hate or revenge, without the desire to hurt merely for the pleasure of hurting. Where man acts according to his own nature in a self-destructive way. In fact, man is essentially murderous in his intent. While animals do not murder. Do not torture. Do not make war on their own species. So whatever he is now, man is not an animal.

And why did God create such a creature knowing what the consequences might be? I did not have the answer. But I thought The Architect might.

It was Monday morning when The Architect called Wild Bill and told him he had discovered the new Jackson Pollock. The artist in question was without finances to paint every day. He was also without structure. Without guidance. Without the figure of a great man to guide him. He needed a home. A place to paint. To be loved for the creature he was born to be—an artist. The sideline of the venture was that Wild Bill could not only become the artist's father figure. He could become his manager. His gallery owner. He could flaunt him around the halls of art society as "Wild Bill's discovery." And with that it was agreed that the Artist would move in with Wild Bill and his Trophy. It was that easy.

CHAPTER 13.

Man versus Alter Ego.

I had a week before I had the deliver the Artist to Wild Bill. I had done my research, my due diligence. I had studied my subject. I took on a new vocabulary, and the words that possessed me were the Artist's. Words like brave … paintings that are brave for the eyes and the heart; confronting … the ultimate priority is a confronting work; naked self … it was about personal exposure and the disappearance of privacy; awful … awful works that people love.

I took myself to the Artist's hometown, the town he had long ago left. I wandered around his old house. I deducted that it must have been designed by a committee of blind lesbians, meaning that everything was there but nothing seemed to be in the right place. Everything about it was functional. It had a front door and a back door. There were rooms divided by big blank pieces of plaster. Cut-out door frames were inserted in the most inappropriate places, making moving from room to room awkward. The roof was just under two meters high. A taller man would have walked with a slump every time he was inside. It had a kitchen with a stove, an oven, a laundry closet. The floor was chipped board. I walked out of the house and vomited. Vomited right on the faded garden gnome set right beside the path that led to this house of horrors. Please don't get me wrong. It was a typical home for the disadvantaged. I just believe that every home, poor or not, can be well designed, designed for life, and not just a place to live and die in.

I cleaned myself up and walked to the rear garden and found the shed the Artist had painted in. Once I lifted the canvas awning against the window I sat and watched the dust fragments dance in the new light that had been let to enter the Artist's old world. The floor was thick with spilled paint and resin, was thick with discarded brushes and paint cans. It had a smell close to sex. It was pungent yet enticing. Strong but not overpowering. The walls were sprayed with the Artist's life: *Playboy* shots of girls that could not be identified, as their faces had been painted over, but their ample breasts were there, ample and on display. Their washboard abs were stripped, their nakedness covered with a randomly placed hand or leaf or cloth. I could smell the scent of escape the Artist smelled here, the pent-up need to succeed. In fact, the more I sat in the room the more the stench for success overcame me. I started to breathe a little shallowly. Then my stomach started to roll and rumble. My forehead started to sweat and bead. I stood groggily and staggered outside. Where I vomited again. I wiped my mouth and staggered to my car. Looking back at the marks of vomit I had left, I saw that it was like I had left my scent to mark the territory in the absence of the Artist.

I drove to the bar the Artist frequented. The people

society had discarded were there, as I was assured. They sat in their dirty jeans and dirty boots. Their ironed shirts. Their slicked-back hair. The crust of sleep still wedged in their eyes. They sat in the semi-darkness the bar provided. In stark contrast to the bright sunny day that welcomed them outside, should they ever decide to leave before dark. I sat next to them and asked what the Artist drank. It was a dirty whisky of sorts.

I watched my new friends. I nudged and coddled my drink as they did. Making small movements every now and then. Using single-word grunts to let them know I was still conscious. The drinks were refilled once the last drops were drained without asking. After five or more drinks I was no longer an outsider; I was a fellow drinker. Once the afternoon started to deepen and the drinks started to take serious effect I began to ask questions. Their responses were varied and different, yet they all contained the same sentiment. The Artist drank to forget what happened inside his house, and yes, the act of painting in his shed made him dream of escape. Those were the two things that echoed again and again. That and the fact the Artist was known to have had a lap-dance favorite. I heard that she might have even retired, but I made my way to the strip club just as dusk was setting anyway. I fumbled my words and raised some stares as I requested a dance from Bev. Some of the young girls came in to stare at me and giggle, pointing at me with their eyes, mocking me with their retreat until a woman in her late forties came in. She was wrinkled in all the right places. The wrinkles defined her, proudly sculpting her face and breasts with the lines of life. "Who's asking to see Bev?" she asked, and I proudly raised my hand like a child asking to answer a question for the teacher.

"I am," I stuttered. Bev circled me once and then twice, looking me up and down. "Well, buy me a drink and let's chat," Bev sprayed in a soft forgiving voice. At least I thought it was Bev.

I sat with Bev and explained my mission to see how the Artist lived, what he saw, what he did, what he felt. And with that Bev took my left hand and placed it roughly on her right breast. She took control of my digits and squeezed her ample cleavage hard and strong. It was the first time I can ever remember feeling a woman's breast. Bev then stood, dropping my hand onto the drinks table. She stood and raised her skirt, tucking it into her waist-band. She turned her face away from me. To hide her disgust? No, so she could roll her fine hips in front of my face. The ripples of muscle and flesh moved to different tunes, but the overall effect was amazing. I wished at that very moment that I could move like that, and that like the Artist, I had witnessed such a private show every day of my earlier life. I even wished for a small moment that I were the Artist. That was until Bev pressed her near-naked ass straight back into my face, pinning my nose high into the crack of her ass. It was like a smack on the nose. My eyes watered on her bright green G-string. Making a wet patch high above where I imagined Bev might be making a wet patch of her own, had I been the Artist. Once my eyes stopped watering I realized that my head was moving to Bev's tune. My head was in perfect rhythm with Bev. No wonder, as my head was so firmly stuck in the crack of her ass I could smell her lunch. And with that Bev let me go. She lowered her skirt, straightening the sides, and then turned to face me. "That's what the Artist felt every day of his life until he stopped coming by."

But why would an Artist stop coming by for this? Bev's voice snapped me back to reality. "That will cost you fifty." And with a lunge into my wallet I produced the credit card The Architect had given me—the company card. Bev laughed harder at my card than the other girls did at me. "Come take a look at this. The Artist's friend wants to pay with a fucking credit card." And with that, more semi-naked girls than I had ever seen before paraded before me. Not laughing at me. They laughed at the card in my hand. "Well, if the man needs to pay by card it's seventy-five dollars!" Bev shrieked and forcibly pulled the card from my hand, and before I knew it she was back with a slimy piece of paper and a pen. My scrawling signature could have been that of anyone's. But it was good enough for Bev.

With that Bev took me through a small passageway marked as "staff only." Once down the narrow walk she opened four small curtains that produced four small viewing windows that looked directly into the four small rooms of the club. Two of the rooms were occupied by girls and their customers. One was having bad missionary sex. The other danced naked. Bev looked at me and explained that the Artist would come there and sketch every night. He sketched the illicit dialogue of the naked body. And with that, all I remember was more drinking followed by more drinking and then waking in the motel with a headache the size of Bev's ass.

I realized that living like an artist was hard work. I realized that it took more than just being a drinker and womanizer to be creative. It took a great disposition for alcohol. A good, firm, strong nose. Both for paint and for Bev's ass.

Now for the story of the Artist and his life, so far, as an artist.

The Artist was handed the baton of creativity and potential greatness long ago. And like his mentor who handed it to him, he dropped it many times along the way. His mentor shall remain nameless, yet he was internationally recognized as one of the greatest living masters of abstract painting.

The mentor convinced the Artist to follow his heart as he painted, and with that the Artist's painting story began. The

Artist followed his fusion of heart to mind. Much was made in art circles of this metaphorical exchange. Romantics flocked to follow the Artist, fascinated by his tender youthfulness and his gregarious talent to engage the audience. His love and knowledge of cooking, of food, added another layer of acceptance by the romantic art crowd.

The Artist had always asked to be handed the baton, and when it was finally surrendered to him it was battered. Broken. Chipped. Yet the Artist maintained that he had the energy and promise to carry it. He planned to carry it for a long time—forever, in his own mind. So he stayed in his shed behind the house of horrors and bench-pressed the baton every day, not taking it outside until he had little option. Until his paintings needed to be shown and sold, so he could continue.

Everyone who saw his large sumptuous works said he was an artist of promise. He was a person on the run to accept the accolades to be praised upon him from atop the art world.

The one who first declared him a brilliant soul, his mentor, taught him an enormous amount. Not only how to look at a subject but how to see through it. Then he taught him how to join the two on a canvas. That advice never left the Artist.

Outside of art the Artist needed a place to forget, away from the bar, away from Bev, a place to hide away. That place was his love of food. Food, glorious food. It could be the Italian take on a ham and cheese panini, a panini that could melt your heart. Or a rustic meal of French, Italian, or Spanish for his table of close friends. For the Artist the colors of food mimicked his palette, his artist's palette. The red of shredded marinated baby beetroot relish, next to the orange of baby carrots. The black ink spagattini resting alongside the wilted baby beetroot leaves. The shiny pod of chili-flaked calamari alongside the burned, salt-crusted fish.

It was like the gritty textures, blurred shapes, and opal like colors helped create an intimate atmosphere good enough to eat. Everything had a place on his plate. It was there that the Artist had the inspiration to paint the dead food that connected the dish on the table.

After actually meeting the Artist I knew he was The Architect's man. How did I know this? The Artist had the "fear of success" tattooed on every piece of his exposed skin. On his forehead. On his arms. His torso. His ass when he showered. His dick when he pissed. He wanted to be applauded and receive the thanks and assurance that what he painted was great and accepted. That he could sustain his painting lifestyle as long as held a brush. He wanted to know that he was a commercial success but more importantly, that he was respected as a painter by his peers. Yet he was also scared to death that one day soon he would have to back up the confidence shown in him. That he would have to do as well or better than was expected of him. Better than his last exhibition. He knew that once on the radar his peers would be watching. The critics would be sniffing around. The buyers and agents would be asking what was next. When would the artist be showing next? How soon? How many? What form?

Yes, the Artist was right for the picking. So I signed him up.

Back at work I wrote a report for The Architect. He scrutinized it like a plan, jotting down notes and doodling. I had never seen him doodle before with words. Before I knew it the finished strategy was drawn. I went through it with the Artist. And in no time at all, The Architect had me, the Assistant, bring the Artist over to Wild Bill's. The Artist trailed me in his well-used truck piled high with canvases. Paint. Brushes. Sticks. Brooms. Mops. Garbage cans drenched in paint.

To Wild Bill there could be nothing sexier than such an animal as an Artist. He effused over the Artist's paraphernalia, salivating at the very thought of the Artist becoming his discovery. He forgot the process and only eyed the goal.

Wild Bill set the Artist up in the bunker or dungeon of his magnificent residence in the darkness of the house. It would be free of distraction. Free of interference. And with that Wild Bill gave the Artist a bed. A clock. Food. A credit card for paint and brushes. Then he was gone. However, he never did warn his Trophy that they now had a houseguest.

On the first day during their first meal together, the Artist started the dinner conversation, asking Wild Bill how much it cost him to have The Architect design for him, for a second time.

"It cost me plenty. Lots of dollars. Maybe more than you will make from the gallery opening."

"It didn't cost you anything else? Just money?"

The question sat lightly on Wild Bill's tongue like a green seeded chili. Not hot enough to spit out but too hot to chew. Wild Bill never told anyone how much his house cost, and would never tell. So what was he really asking?

"Did you buy a partner or a master?"

"I bought a master architect. A designer who would push me to live differently in one of his creations."

"So you would alter the way you live to live with beauty?"

"I have you here, don't I?"

Before Wild Bill could chew his chili further, the Artist continued.

"So who will The Architect bring in next? Once I have gone?"

Wild Bill was now open-jawed. He had no idea where this was heading. But he had to have the last word; after all it was his house.

"I will decide who enters my home. Not The Architect. Not Trophy. And not you!"

The Artist felt Wild Bill's temper. So he jumped in again.

"How does a man like you, Wild Bill, build his own home? Does he build it for himself? For his own quirks, to be uniquely his? A man's own home must be a home that will never wear out. Never grow old. Never fall down. It must be capable of lasting indefinitely. It must have spiritual significance. Because man is not a creature of spiritual insignificance himself; he is a unique creature and is dependent upon the structure of his body and his spirit. It is wrong to think of a man's body as incidental. If he did, then the man might have the neck of a giraffe or the body of a pig. Meaning no man and his body are instantly designed to fulfill the role for which he was created. We must all adapt. We must all learn. We must all be helped to reach our final goal, by God or similar. In my case, by you, Wild Bill." And with that the Artist scraped the last of his dinner from his plate, telling everyone he would clean up as part of his board, and went down to his dungeon.

I will stop the Artist right here. We all know that Wild Bill's house was amazing, and the dungeon as the Artist called it was not a dungeon to be scoffed at. Let me describe "the dungeon" for you just so you get the picture. Yes, it was underground. Yes, it was cement construction. But it was Japanese aerated concrete, cast on site. The white Dalsouple natural rubber floor had below-ground heating. It was air-conditioned, temperature-controlled. Humidity was monitored and evened. It housed a small shower and toilet, more like a bathroom in a small hotel room. It had a laundry in an enclosed cupboard. It had towels, packs of soap, shampoos and conditioners, skin lotion in small pre-packed tubes. It had little natural light, so to create mood and shadows, the Artist had decided to use small "kino flow/neon-like lights" on long cables that snaked from the power points. He would use them to create the shadow and highlight he wanted. He would use them like he was God, playing with the sun and the cloud in his own sky. He would use the rain from the sink like he was God. He would use the wind machine like he was God, blowing everything in its path to destruction. Yes, the Artist was God of his own dungeon. So why would he question Wild Bill? Why would he look a gift horse, like Wild Bill, in the mouth? It was because success was on its way. It was close. He could smell it. And it scared him to death.

The Artist went underground to digest his dinner while Wild Bill kept the questions on his tongue for a while longer before he too continued to eat, although he could not erase the same question from his mind: "Why in God's name would the Artist question me, Wild Bill, his benefactor, his patron?"

Trophy continued to eat throughout the whole event. Then out of the blue the Artist came back into the kitchen and asked the question Wild Bill had never even imagined.

"Could I use Trophy as the subject matter for my next series of paintings?" It sprang from the Artist's mouth like a flying piece of broccoli.

Wild Bill spoke with his mouth half empty. "Of course. As long as Trophy is happy to play along."

Trophy kept eating, still not listening to words she thought did not concern her. So Wild Bill answered for her. "Then I guess from the lack of resistance it's a done deal."

And with that dinner rolled along until its end. The dishes were cleared, and then the Artist volunteered his services to cook every meal from the next day on to show his thanks for becoming part of Wild Bill's family. Everyone agreed. The

Artist went downstairs to his quarters below the house and with that knowledge in place started to sketch.

As the Artist sketched he paused to open Wild Bill's commercial freezer located in his dungeon, dragging out the dead animals he had hidden there. He brought them into the house wrapped in plastic.

Pulling away the plastic, the Artist laid them out. All of them sat curled up and rested just the way he had left them. The Artist let them sit in the controlled comfort of his dungeon and watched them thaw. They thawed until he could manhandle them. He sat them up and manhandled their heads until they cracked a little, until he pointed their eyes to his gaze. He moved their fur, brushing it sometimes, keeping its grain running in the right direction. As they began to thaw further the Artist stood them up. Moving their hind legs in such a way to represent sexuality. I know we may differ here. Sexuality of an animal? But the weight of his composition, with the dead animals, was meaningful and recognizable on a subliminal level, at least for me. All I wondered was where Trophy would fit in.

Chapter 14.

Erection. Masculinity. Divorce.

Wild Bill exercised daily in the gym near to the Artist's dungeon. He got up at six. Did a twelve-kilometer run. Then stretched. Hit the weights for forty-five minutes. Stretched again. Showered and went down to breakfast in the kitchen.

Let me explain the kitchen, because Wild Bill's was not just any old kitchen. And from today onward it was to be possessed by a passionate artist.

Wild Bill's kitchen had Hagenau and Thermoform. A Garland salamander overhead broiler and a built-in panini maker. Wood. Steel. Marble. Aluminum. Chromed metal. Graphite frosted glass. It had primary design depicted by its lack of handles and geometric surfaces. Matrix composition. Island unit. Double worktop in steel with soldered steel sinks. The rear of the island housed fridges, full and empty units to highlight the elements of the program matrix. There were three ovens. The range hood system housed an integrated lighting system. And everything was glacier white. Everything incidental was hidden. Not visible. The pullout storage included a cutlery canteen, knife racks, spice holders, and basins. All the steel surfaces had a special treatment to make them refractory to stains and fingerprints. You get the picture.

Then there were the ultimate bits and pieces that sat proudly on display: the spoon scale, a spoon with a built-in scale accurate to within one-tenth of a gram. It would have been perfect for dealing out drugs. There was the set of "mood" bottle openers, faces painted onto each opener. There was Mr. Happy, Sad, Crazy, and Shocked.

The Louis Vuitton cooking apron sat beside a cupboard next to the hot, not too hot, and cold mugs. Yes, the ones that said COLD in big black letters until you added the hot beverage, causing the mug to change color and read HOT.

There were the perfect martini glasses created by AlissiaMT known to every design aficionado out there for their collection of diamond rings.

And last but not least there was the world's most expensive knife. At $39,000 you could buy a car with the money spent on this knife. Designed by a renowned jewelry artist in collaboration with blade smiths Hoffman/Pieper, it was as sharp as it was glamorous. With a Damascus steel patter, scrimshaw and engraving, individually inscribed.

Breakfast from that day onward in Wild Bill's house was to be an experience.

The Artist's love of cooking came from the diner his mother worked at. He watched the ethnic cooks prepare the food. Peel it. Cook it. Mix it with color and spice. Take it from starchy to runny to velvety smooth. The work in the kitchen and the work in his studio were closely connected. Yes, there was flavor and process that came from painting and cooking.

But right now was breakfast time, the most important meal of the day.

When Wild Bill entered the kitchen his nose had entered it meters prior. The smell of rustic breakfast molecules had triggered the neurons and cilia in his nose before he could witness seeing every brand name in his kitchen working. The Gaggenau was humming. The Thermador was keeping the Artist's concoction chilled. The salamander and panini maker had worked their magic, and Wild Bill was suddenly ravenous. The Artist had set places on the stainless steel bench that sat in front of the graphite frosted glass. The food sat like a still life about to be photographed before the eighteenth-century guests devoured every bit of it, eating with their hands as if the convention of knives and forks was too hard to comprehend. Yes, Wild Bill was mighty impressed. He looked at the breakfast and was amazed. Colors ran like a squashed rainbow on his kitchen bench, and suddenly Wild Bill's hand was occupied by a glass of fluorescent green liquid. The Artist, who did not drink, toasted Wild Bill, who drank heavily. The green liquid seemed to calm Wild Bill like never before. It seemed to coat his throat and soothe his senses. For the first time Wild Bill was at ease about the Artist living in his home. The Artist enquired about Trophy and what time she would come down to breakfast. But he was fobbed off with excuses about her never eating breakfast, never getting up early, not being an early riser. So after they ate, the Artist cleaned the geometric surfaces like his life depended on it. Which it did. He rinsed everything in the soldered steel sinks. Double-checked that the three ovens were off and on self-clean. Then he bid Wild Bill good morning and left for his dungeon to wait for Trophy.

The Artist pictured what Trophy might look like in her lingerie with her top half down, her hand positioned across her breast, hiding her pink nipple, and with that he started to get an erection. Which in this instance was professionally irresponsible. So he stopped it. You see, an erection goes hand in hand with virility, and Wild Bill had more than enough testosterone and virility for this house and most probably the whole street. Virility—it was something only the male species had. Virility was essentially associated with the "fathering of children." And strangely enough, Wild Bill and Trophy had no children.

As virility is to men, fertility is to women. So was Trophy unripe? The Artist had no clue. Maybe Trophy was all fucked out. Maybe Wild Bill had exhausted her with his unwanted sexual activity and virility, with his masculinity dripping from every sweat pore. Maybe Trophy was over the pumped-up physique. The hairy back. Maybe all she wanted was to be appreciated for who she was. Maybe. Maybe, instead of a god, Trophy wanted a hero—something Wild Bill had forgotten the meaning of.

A subnote here: Whenever a woman is mentioned a man's character will always be judged, and along with his character, what he stands for. Remember The Architect and Mia? Remember Adam and Eve? Now it was the Artist's turn with Trophy. Oh, one more thing. Even in ancient times one rule stood out, one rule used to judge all men on. It read, "If a man takes a woman to wife but he has no loving intercourse with her, this woman is no wife to him."

With Trophy on his mind the Artist removed himself from his dungeon and sat on the veranda nearest the kitchen with an open view of the sitting room, near to the study. And he watched with his peripheral vision while he waited for Trophy and sketched. The Artist sketched not from his surrounding but from memories and projections. The Artist did not have to meditate to have projections; they rained down on him whenever he let them. And now he let them. The Artist sketched pencil on paper with a sense of urgency. He sketched with conviction, with a new lease of life, one he had lost a time ago. The Artist sketched until Trophy walked in.

Breathe. Breathe … Sorry, I have let myself run away. We must go back to the group. To the Chairman. To the group in the small meeting room. They are waiting for us.

CHAPTER 15.

It's Getting Hot in Here.

I had done all the explaining, but Wild Bill looked exhausted, drained, spent. He looked hot after his marathon in front of the group. Hot under the collar. And he was right. The room we all met in was not air-conditioned. The chairs were hot and sweaty. There were windows, but there was no consideration for cross-flow. All there was, was a water cooler. And we each took it in turns, grabbing a plastic cup and filling our cup slowly when the air in the room stuck to us like hot toffee. When the story got too harrowing. When one's inner self was exposed. When someone had their pants around their ankles and their dick swinging in the wind.

Wild Bill's story had been just that, even to Wild Bill, who pushed past us to grab a handful of weak plastic cups. Squashing most of them in his attempt to fill them with ice-cold water to drown his sore, thirsty throat with the cold

97

liquid. Yes, we were not yet halfway through the night. It was summer. It was freaking hot. And we all had a long way to go. The Architect had touched all our lives, and tonight was the night every story would be told. The one night everyone would tell all.

Which caused me to remember the first night I sat with The Architect in his control room. It was also summer, last summer. I had queued up all of the video feeds from the cameras at their juiciest parts, ready to press play for The Architect. Yes, you guessed it, I was finally certified as chief hall monitor, and it was my job to look for incriminating footage and then draw up a punishment sheet. The punishments ranged in severity from one to ten, eight being time for intervention, but not in a traditional sense, more like the Artist coming in to Wild Bill's house. More like someone to come in and sort things out, set things straight, like the rats. On the scale sheet of punishment the least severe was a one, meaning small electrical shocks like Bruce had to endure.

I remember that first summer night when The Architect came in. The room temperature was a balmy twenty-three. The air-conditioner fan purred on low; the push of air it created was little more than a cool breath, detectable, but only just. The dimmer controlling the twelve-watt LED recessed dimmable downlights was on about 20 percent. The quality of light was something you would expect from an incandescent, which made the LED video screens pop. Yes, pop. They popped with color. But the real pop was the recorded action.

The Architect sat and watched his clients commit crimes against architecture. Blatant crimes against good design. Against great color combinations. Against the very contract they had all signed with The Architect. Then they all committed the most outrageous crime of all. They blasphemed against the very person they each begged to design their project: The Architect. Some made a passing comment while others made it personal.

The Architect sat there and watched each video. He replayed some of them—some three times or more—yet he never strayed from looking at the screens. His face grew redder in color. His neck started to flower in roseola. Yes, kissing disease. But The Architect had not had sex for years. The rash became an intricate inkblot. I studied his face and his pores to determine personality characteristics and emotional functioning. The weekend inkblot course I took via correspondence confirmed my thinking. The Architect was pissed. Pissed off. Cranky. Furious. He viewed the very last screen and asked me for my recommendations—my punishment recommendations! I glowed with pride. I glowed with the opportunity to whoop some ass. He looked down and smiled, smirked a little, like the puppet master he was. Then he raised his head and smiled at me again. He looked at me through the smile and said, "Thank you. Thank you. Thank you." He knew he was in good hands.

The Architect left the room. Then he did what he'd never done before. He put his head back into the room and smiled at me again. Obviously I knew what this meant. I looked down at the punishment forms and drew the only conclusion I could. I had ticked the punishment boxes at "seven," but his smile made me change my mind. He made me see the light in all the darkness. I knew I had to change the scores to eight. And I thanked him for it. I think he may have left the office before I said it, but I said it anyway.

So from that day onward, I would become the watcher *and* the punisher. No one would escape me. I would check every morning and every night. I set my alarm by the waking patterns of the biggest nonconformist. Nothing was to escape my due diligence for repercussion, because for every action there was to be a reaction.

And that is just what happened to Wild Bill. Having stood in front of all of us for so long his actions and his words made him tired. Hot and tired. He must have drunk a lot of the Artist's brew. A lot. Because for the first time Wild Bill looked less of a man. In fact the whole group looked exhausted. It was early evening. We had been telling our tales about The Architect for almost eight hours, and we would continue for however long it took to purge ourselves.

So while the others were having a breather, slouching in the ugly chairs that ate us, let me tell you about the first time The Architect gave me a job of my own to design and finish. Yes, a job of my own.

It was a design project made in heaven—not architectural design; it was more interior design. I know. Please do not tsk tsk me. Interior design is important.

My client was rich beyond normal comprehension. The house had already been designed and built, but not by The Architect, so I am certain that's why he gave the project to me. The house had cost eighty million dollars. Yes, you heard right. And what do you get for eighty million dollars? Let me show off what money gets you. You get a walk-in cigar humidor, the kind made by Michael Perrenoud from Switzerland, the kind that holds ten thousand cigars.

You get walls cloaked in timber paneling, touched by velvet and gold drapes. Surrounded by pieces of art that belonged in museums. I could go on ad nauseam about the walls of calfskin and Chinese onyx. The cascading waterfall. The twenty-four hour butlers. The butlers' quarters. The midair spa baths. Hundreds of surveillance cameras. Now that's something I was familiar with. Bulletproof windows. Armored doors. Bedside panic buttons. The 1930's billiard table. The Steinway grand. The intimate dining room for twenty-eight. Six bathrooms. Poker table. Fully equipped gym. Wet bar. Media room. Jacuzzi. Pool. Sauna and spa treatment room. The eight-foot round bed with mirrored ceiling. The half-court basketball workout room with the separate locker room. The glass fireplace by Bloch. Digital picture frame by Hyundai. Panic room, as the brochure says, for the rich and scared, constructed with reinforced steel sheeting and eight-inch concrete walls. A Kharma Hi-Fi system came in at a miserly one million dollars. There was the Swarovski crystal-studded toilet and fridge. The home heater system by Frankentek. I could go on and on, but that is not my task. My task was to design for three rooms, the lounge, dining room, and bedroom; to design furniture with the client's needs in mind. You see, the client and his friends were nudists. Naturalists.

So my first and thought was see-through furniture. Transparent chairs. Desks. Lounge suites. Bed covers, and Duvet's. You see, interior design is not about the ordinary. In this case it was all about the extraordinary.

The lounge room and dining rooms were the easiest. For the dining room I took one of The Architect's finest dining chair designs, with his permission of course, and had it recast in a special Plexiglas compound. The Plexiglas artisans hand-shaped the chair design and then cast multiples of them, hand-producing twenty-eight chairs in total. Hand-polishing them all.

Just to be sure I was doing the right thing I took a prototype home and sat my camera directly under the chair on the floor. Then I proceeded to remove all my clothes and hit record. I sat on the chair. Wiggling my ass. I stood. Then re-sat. Fast and slowly. I hit record at a thousand frames per second. I sat cross-legged. I sat closed-legged and open-legged. The results were unbelievable. I watched the tape over and over, scrutinizing every part of the footage. The footage that captured every dangle, every loose piece of flesh, every look at my chocolate starfish, and I decided that in the not-too-distant future I would have a ball-bag tuck. Yes, after this adventure it was inevitable. Or else I would live with the air temperature at a cool sixteen degrees so my ball-bag crawled up to hug my body, relieving the sagging skin that sat there.

The next room I worked on was the lounge room. The shape of a sofa or lounge was easy. Be it French provincial. Art deco. Modern. Georgian. Or Victorian. The shape I chose was modern and was molded. It, too, was formed in see-through Plexiglas. It was the comfort factor that had me stumped for a short time, same with the master bedroom and the request for a see-through duvet. And then it hit me. I took Cling Wrap as my base component and filled it with hot air and then sealed it. It was a warm, light pillow of air. I researched clear plastic and had my technical design team recreate plastic with silicone nodules, and then I transferred it to the Nanotechnology Department. They used the infill-cell treatment and molded the exterior of the see-through lounge cushions and duvet cover and formed a cell of hot air. The lounge cushions and duvet were connected to a pump that continually pumped warm air into the cell, creating the constant temperature I desired. A thermostat device was connected to warm the air in winter and cool the air cell in summer. And it was see-through. Wipe proof. Sanitized. Everything my nudist client ordered.

I was invited to the housewarming. The bed-warming. The sofa-warming. But as someone who now frowns at seeing themselves naked in the fogged bathroom mirror, I declined. Besides, I already had the one thousand frame slow motion test of the chocolate starfish. And that stopped me from eating chocolate for weeks.

I can hear the group shuffling around their fat chairs. So it must be time to head back. Oh, oh stand by. Bruce is insisting he get back up.

CHAPTER 16.

Bruce Retakes the Stand.

There was fighting and shoving in the room. Wild Bill was being held back by The President of The Island while Bruce was looking down at his shoes, scratching at the floor with his feet like a fighting rooster. Scratching and clawing that floor until there were marks in it like furrows cut by wild toenails.

Bruce was demanding. Demanding that it was his turn to speak. He had so much to say. It was evening already. And he wanted his turn.

So it was agreed to. Reluctantly.

The President of The Island let go of Wild Bill's arm, and calm seemed to be restored. Bruce stood in front of us as awkward as ever. Only this time he also had remnants of food spilled down his shirt. And there were tongue marks on it, where he had tried to lick up the sweet and sour Chinese sauce that had dripped off his mini dim sum, the one he double-dipped. And we all know you can never take a bite and double-dip. But that was not the last we were going to hear about food, parties, and dripping sauce.

Bruce started to tell us about his housewarming. Yes, Bruce had all our ears, and we were going to hear every detail of his housewarming. One of us groaned, but all would soon be enthralled by what we were about to hear.

Bruce's housewarming invitation was in no way lavish, in no way ostentatious. The invitation was a phone call. The first call was to The Architect; in fact, I intercepted it on his behalf. The date was the eighth. A Saturday. I scanned The Architect's diary, and of course it was free. Every day except for work was free; he had no life outside this office. So I told Bruce I would confirm closer to the eighth. As the eighth was nearing I actually asked The Architect if he wanted to attend. He looked at me shyly for a while. Then blurted out the one thing I didn't know about Bruce.

"I would if he wasn't so codependent."

I had not diagnosed that about Bruce previously. But now it was perfectly clear to me. You see, codependents are needy. Demanding. Submissive. They cling to others and act immaturely. Codependents also appear to be impervious to abuse. No matter how badly they are mistreated, they remain committed. So with that in mind, I sadly said no to Bruce.

Bruce offered to come by and collect The Architect for the party if it was the four-hour drive each way that was putting him off. He offered to let The Architect have his bed if he wanted to sleep over. But no groveling would change The Architect's no. So I offered to come in The Architect's place. To fly the flag. And Bruce begrudgingly accepted.

The eighth was a beautiful desert day. Ninety degrees Fahrenheit in the day and seventy-eight degrees Fahrenheit in the night. The invited guests were as I expected. Bruce. Myself.

Two of the main building contractors, the electrician, who probably came along just to make sure no one got electrocuted by those mysterious shocks, and the steel fabricator; who was an alcoholic and never said no to a drink. Plus the ten Mexican laborers who had worked tirelessly on his house.

To reinforce that the interior of his stunning low-slung desert home was off-limits. To make sure no one would scratch The Architect's vision. Bruce had designated viewing hours, so the housewarming guests could walk through his masterpiece in broad daylight, with Bruce as guide. They were held in fifteen-minute intervals. One person at a time. He had a rug on the floor. And everyone had to take off their shoes before they went inside. The electrical contractor was first. He brought his meter with him and dutifully confirmed that the building was safe. Then everyone had their time to appreciate the wonder of Bruce's low-slung house. Marvel at its simplicity. And Bruce's courage to live so far from anywhere.

By nightfall the canapés, or food as Bruce called them. Had been consumed and leftovers were put back in the very same plastic containers they came in and stored in Bruce's fridge. To be used as leftover meals for another day. And that's when the drinking started. The laborers started with ice-cold silver bullets, beers to the uninitiated. It was hot I confess, but they drank Bruce's silver bullets like their lives depended on it. Then they drank Bruce's toasting champagne. In fact it was not champagne, as it was not French. It was sparkling wine. From the new Amercias. From Chile. So Bruce was making out that they were snarfing his prized champagne while all they were doing was washing their shirts in cheap Chilean sparkling wine as they spilled it from their mouths to their torso. They passed around the two bottles. Yes, two miserly bottles passed around from mouth to mouth. Bruce got his mouthful when he grabbed a bottle off the biggest laborer who momentarily stared Bruce in the face as if he were a rattlesnake about to bite him, but after Bruce swigged from the bottle and nearly choked, coughing up all the champagne he had in his mouth, dropping to his knees like a soft cock that he was, the big laborer looked at his comrades and laughed. He laughed and laughed. Bruce finally stopped coughing as he lay in the desert dirt. His face and blue button-up shirt covered in wet dirt. The laborers danced around him, pointing and laughing. And that's when Bruce left his own party to watch the mayhem from the small hill that sat due north from the house. It was also when the electrician decided to go, waving good-bye to Bruce on the hill. Bruce watched the laborers and the steel fabricator drink all of his prized champagne and then open their private stash of tequila. Bruce categorically told them there was to be no additional alcohol on the premises, and they all agreed on the phone. He believed them, and it was this belief that stopped him from searching each and every one's bag as they arrived. But now he regretted it. He regretted it even more as the drunk laborers brought out the rows and rows of firecrackers along with their bottles of trouble.

The door to his magnificent house was barricaded with stolen police-barricade tape. It was super-strength tape and designed with bright police colors to highlight all the Keep Out and Do Not Cross signs. As a weakling threatened by authority, Bruce hoped it would have the same effect on the laborers as it had on him. It did seem to have the desired effect on the alcoholic steel fabricator, who lay outside Bruce's door like a sleeping dog on guard.

But before he could take back his house Bruce had to contend with the firecrackers. As well as loud bangs, the laborers stash included some terrific rockets that whizzed when they left the earth and exploded when they hit the upper atmosphere at the very apex of their journey.

The smell of gunpowder became a little intoxicating and seemed to make Bruce forget exactly where he was for a minute as he sat on the small hill due north of his house. It seemed to make him forget his current troubles while the rainbow of colors exploded above him. The colors meshed with the black sky. And Bruce thought what a wonderful color black was. So giving. So happy to be in the background. While the other colors ran and smudged all over it. Bruce thought that black was a little like him. And from that day on Bruce decided to only wear black. A bad decision really, as he lived in the heat of the desert and the color black would absorb every ounce of heat it could ingest. But Bruce didn't worry about that.

The laborers let off all their rockets. All their roman candles that created stars and bombettes. All their fountains that showered golden glows. All their waterfalls that spewed vertical curtains of sparks. It was only when one of the single-shot crackers left the hand of its laborer and flew into the open window of Bruce's palace by mistake that things really turned sour. The single-shot cracker sat on the floor of Bruce's low-slung masterpiece as if it was deciding whether to explode or not. No one outside the house realized where it had gone until they heard the mighty echo of explosion. All heads turned to the source of the noise. Bruce's house.

The noise startled a wild fox that had stood rather close to Bruce on the next small hilltop. Before the explosion it seemed to look at Bruce with a sad face that said, "Poor animal. I feel sorry for you." Bruce had eyeballed it, and just as he was going to agree, the mighty explosion from inside scared it off into the night. Bruce asked himself whether he would ever see that fox again.

The laborers were amazed that the very house they had helped build was the perfect amphitheater for sound. A perfect magnifier. So they stopped throwing the single-shot crackers into the wide-open unknown and instead threw them selectively into the house they built. Bruce was mortified. He was frozen. Scared. He pressed his hands close to his ears to stop the sound of the explosions. But his hands could not cup his ears sufficiently to negate the sound of fun, nor the laborers laughs and cackles that also filtered through his fingers as they oohed and aahed between crackers. Bruce could not take it any longer, so he skulked down over the hill he was on and moved his legs with the help of his hands, step by step, to a bank in the hidden hillside where he found a small hole in the side of the wall. Bruce crawled into it and retreated into the fetal position. Waiting for the noise to stop and the alcohol to take its effect.

Scared that I was going to miss something, I remembered that the motion sensors in The Architect's media closet would have alerted the automated recording device of Bruce's party. So I could replay things a million times. But what I witnessed with my own eyes sent shivers so far up my spine that they reverberated in my teeth. I was uncertain if it was a shiver of pleasure. Or pain.

Eventually, after every cracker and explosion had had their day, the laborers lay down on the floor of The Architect's magnificent building and fell asleep. I looked down at my empty palm as if it were a punishment sheet and I could not see a number that sufficiently correlated to the pain Bruce was about to feel. It was his house. His house to protect. And he had not protected it sufficiently.

I thought about Bruce a lot that night on my four-hour drive home and decided that in a funny, messy sort of way, Bruce could have been the perfect client. When The Architect designed Bruce's house he didn't have to worry about freeways. Neighborhoods. Bus stops. Schools. Corner shops. Transport grids. Sidewalks. Traffic. Garbage collections. Street sweeping. The police force. Or noise. All he had to worry about was Bruce.

I went straight to the office Monday morning and prepared the video screens of Bruce's party and was trying to pick the right time to show The Architect when Bruce walked into the door of the office. I was stunned. I looked at him and had to bite my tongue until it bled to stop myself from chastising him. Instead I asked how he thought his party went, and with that invitation Bruce asked to meet with The Architect—immediately—to ask him to design an extension to his house for guests. I was explaining that that might not be such a great idea when The Architect walked in to the room. Bruce walked up to The Architect, invaded his personal space, and splattered his face with spittle before I could intercept. I managed to grab his arm and pull him slightly away to let The Architect wipe his face with his tissue before he answered. Bruce's request was simple. He needed guest accommodation. He needed it regardless of the fact that it did not connect—may not connect—would not connect with the main building. He wanted, demanded, that the Architect design him an extension, a pod, a standalone outhouse, whatever The Architect wanted to call it. Bruce demanded it.

The Architect stood there slightly bemused. I could tell by the way his pupils dilated, squeezing up into tiny balls of black right in the center of his eyes, like a sphincter muscle trying to hold in diarrhea. The pressure behind the eye was immense. I just hoped it would not create a brain aneurysm, a ballooning of the artery behind the eye, due to the immense pressure The Architect must have been channeling. But it did not. Thank God. The Architect smiled a half smile in Bruce's direction and said he would consider it. And with that he disappeared.

I fumbled a babbling Bruce out the door.

As he sauntered away I could sense that Bruce was filled with his usual demeanor. He was wearing his lack of confidence. His low self-worth. He wore an overcoat of tiredness. His breath smelled of abandonment. He also wore black clothes for the first time. But nothing could prepare him for The Architect's upcoming wrath. You see, I felt that the time was right for The Architect to see the lowlights of the party Bruce had held in The Architect's house, so I ran a hard cable from the media room to The Architect's work area. I had a clam-shell monitor in my hand. I hit play, and the cattle call of footage literally stopped The Architect mid-chew. Thank God his mouth did not fall open and spill his breakfast on the beautiful hummingbird drawings.

The Architect had me rewind the footage twenty or thirty times. He moved himself closer to the screen, moving his eye line from foreground to background and back. And all he said to me was, "Is that Bruce siting on the hill?" I confirmed his suspicion. Then he looked at me, and I jumped out of the starting box like a greyhound.

"Punishment. Bruce has it coming does he not?" The Architect smiled at me and left. I knew what he meant by that smile and what I had to do. I had to punish Bruce. The Architect slipped back into my room as I was writing down a suitable punishment to match the suitable crime.

"You go ahead and design the extension. But make it something Bruce would never expect."

I marked the punishment sheet at ten. Then I put it aside as I laid out my paper. My pencil. I had to lay out my plan and design Bruce his guest accommodation.

First I had to research Bruce thoroughly. I had to know my client intimately before I could design a meaningful extension. I chose his psychologist. It wasn't hard to prevaricate. In fact it was easy. I had prevaricated my whole life to get out of trouble. And now it was a necessary deceive to gain the information I required.

Nothing I discovered from Bruce's psychologist surprised me. Bruce was indeed codependent. And yes he was needy. Submissive. Demanding. He suffered from anxiety and abandonment just like The Architect said. I found out that Bruce was abandoned as a child. Found in a shoebox with a sheet wrapped over him. He lived in twenty-eight different foster homes and fell in love with each and every new mother he had. He would not piss unless they were holding his hand. He loved being the victim.

The psychologist told me that Bruce had kept the very sheet he was found in and slept with it to this day. It was still unwashed after forty-something years—unwashed with the stains and smell of placenta on it, and that's where I got my idea for Bruce's extension.

I went back to the office and started to draw, more like a seagull than a hummingbird, but I was in a hurry. I drew and I drew. Then I went shopping and decided to make a model of my creation.

I drove in my little car on Saturday morning to Bruce's magnificent house to show him what he had purchased. It was not a pod, not a cube; it was a tent. A tent set around a box-like shape. A shoebox-like space with a flapping tent cover. The tent cover had a subtle camouflage design in subtle smeared blood-red tones. Yes, the tent was a larger version the shoebox Bruce was found in. The flapping walls of the tent were designed to emulate the flapping sheet that covered his naked body as a baby. And once Bruce set eyes on it he flipped. Literally. Flipped out.

Bruce put his hands to his ears and ran around screaming. He ran around in small steps. He ran around in perfect concentric circles. He ran around so many times that the pattern he created on the desert floor was imprinted. It was a sight to behold. But Bruce did not appreciate it. I captured it on my phone camera just after Bruce headed for the hills. I saw him disappear over the small hill he had sat on to watch his party from hell. And I never saw him again.

But I did shout out the name of my creation, for his new guest accommodation, just in the hope that he had stopped screaming; I called it Placenta Haven. And with that I left. I left with my model. I left Bruce to his own devices so I could implement the first stages of construction of Placenta Haven.

On my return to The Architect's office I was bubbling with enthusiasm. I bounded in and searched for The Architect. He was in some sort of trance. My vocal interjection did not even startle him, but he did raise his hand to stop me. He then pushed a gold filleted brochure toward me. I picked it up, and the headline jumped out at me. It read, "The Bi-Annual Design Competition for Elite Architects of the World. Invitation Only."

Chapter 17.

The Competition Heats Up.

The Architect was getting tired of the distractions: the Bruce's, the President, Wild Bill.

All he pined for was architecture. All he wanted was to confront the saying "Was it art or was it design?" And the best way to push the boundaries was the invitation only, "Bi-Annual Design Competition for Elite Architects of the World."

The competition name was a bigger mouthful than even Trophy had endured. But it meant The Architect could focus entirely on the competition, entirely on design, while I ran the office.

The first few days the office was so quiet that I watched The Architect from afar. Further away than normal so as not to disturb him, not to disturb his design. His design was going to be unique.

Let me explain the competition brief to give you the overall premise. The competition gurus invite architects, engineers, designers, and artists from around the globe to take part in the world's most prestigious award for residential architecture. The award recognizes approaches that redefine residential design through novel technologies, materials, aesthetics, and spatial organization. It was also the leading light toward exploration and adaption of new habitats based on the dynamic equilibrium between man and nature, all based around intelligent growth.

Registration was based on a CV, a résumé, and a one hundred thousand dollar entry check. It could be an individual entry or a team entry. Submission requirements were set in stone or onscreen.

Because this competition was meant to save the world, there were no hard copies. It was all to be online. Project submissions must include plans, sections, perspectives, and a project statement.

Judges included the 2010 Winner of the Bi-Annual Design Competition for Elite Architects of the World, principals of the world's great architectural firms, professors, associate professors. The green brigade. The visionary brigade.

The Architect hand-wrote his mission statement on his wall in black marker. It read, "Architecture in a Protected Natural Environment." The he scribbled in smaller writing, "Water sensitive. Organic shapes. Complex geometry." With this The Architect started. He ordered me to find him translucent balls. Large balls. Small balls. Balls with dimples. Smooth balls. Bubbles. Moon-shaped balls. Balls for playing rugby. Soccer. Basketball. Volleyball. Yes, The Architect already knew a lot about balls. Then he had me get a hose attached to a water bottle. A bong. Yes, a bong.

He asked me, "What were circles made up of?"

I answered, "a circle is a simple shape of Euclidean

geometry. Simple closed curves dividing the plane into two regions, interior and exterior. It's the boundary of the figure, or the whole figure, including the interior. It's a set of points in a plane that are a given distance from the center. The distance between any point and the center is the radius."

He smiled. "Now cut the bottom off the circle, and what do you have?"

"You have a dome."

"I am thinking about a geodesic dome."

A geodesic dome is a spherical or partial-spherical structure. It was around 1948 that the term "tensegrity" was applied to such a dome. Tensegrity was a principle of continuous tension and discontinuous compression that allowed a dome lightweight lattice and interlocking icosahedrons, which could be skinned. Skinned to provide a protective cover. Spheres enclose the greatest volume for the least surface area, you know.

And this is what The Architect already knew. He also knew that geodesic constructions, even though appearing to be round, have a large number of edges—more than conventional buildings. And each edge must be prevented from leaking, especially in The Architect's design, which was going to challenge even The Architect. He was going to bypass the usual structural material used in a dome—no concrete, no steel, no normal timber.

You see, the construction of this timber grid shell started with a flat two-dimensional wooden net. The structure was achieved by pushing, or forming shape into the intended end result. The Architect was going to do just that by raising two flat wooden nets. But not from wood as you would expect. The Architect chose bamboo for internal and external nets and support to follow the dome shape, to surf underneath it, to surf above it, not touching it, anchoring it only to the ground. His material needed to be natural. Sustainable. So

The Architect chose this bamboo, this grass. Yes, in reality, this bamboo was indeed a grass, a grass called Guadua. His technical studies showed that it had superior mechanical properties. He called it "vegetable steel." You see, bamboo only possesses a small proportion of lignin; its main component is silicic acid, which allows bamboo and Guadua to absorb energy with far greater bending strength.

To cloak the dome itself The Architect first looked at lightweight recycled glass. Imagine a contact lens. A contact lens big enough to live in. Then he started testing polycarbonate, which is lighter than normal plastic. It blocks UV rays and is shatter resistant, and he could add ultraviolet protection via a coating. It all seemed to fit. The Architect had the essence of his design.

Then he asked if there was such a thing as artificial water. I knew there wasn't; artificial water was just the same components of real water put back together, usually with an igniter to develop a fuel. So I offered up the possibility of salt water. Seawater. If the earth was warming and the icecaps melting, there was even more of the stuff. It was actually becoming too abundant. With that he kissed me on the forehead. Then he asked me to research jets, water jets, to see how water deluge systems normally used in special hazard systems work.

I researched nozzles—high-velocity, medium-velocity, and low-velocity nozzles. He asked me to look at "wet pipe sprinkler systems." And right to the very end I had no idea why, no idea until he showed me his hummingbird drawings for his design. It was a globe. A polycarbonate globe with a skeleton of Guadua bamboo. The exterior skeleton, being bamboo, was the perfect wet pipe, because it was hollow. The perfect hose. The Guadua bamboo was to be filled with seawater pumped straight from the ocean. And it would spray the outside of The Architect's house. It would spray it via deluge nozzles. The nozzles would create a screen, a screen so you could walk around the house naked, a screen to have a shower under. Let me explain. The nozzles were positioned all over the bamboo skeleton facing straight down on the polycarbonate dome and localized. The interior rooms were rooms like in a conventional house. The roof of which was transparent. No blinds. No coverings. The seawater was the blind. Turn it on to have a shower. The ensuing spray on the polycarbonate roof concealed the image below. It also acted as a cooling agent in summer. At night, once off, the polycarbonate dome becomes a star-gazing room. And with that The Architect shooed me away so he could do his own technical plans. Perspectives. A mission statement.

With that I had little to do again.

The office was quiet. Silent. The dust in the air fell heavily on the desktop. It seemed to be weighing my hair down, my head down. It seemed to cast a dark dust cloud over my thoughts. So I did what everyone does when they are quiet. I looked at my computer. I scrolled through my personal photos. The photos that meant something only to me. Christmas. New Year's. My birthday. The birthday shots were the last time I had spent with friends.

Work with The Architect had taken over my life. I turned the digital page on my next lot of birthday photos and saw the one photo that today meant more to me than anything. It was a photo of my birthday cake, a slice of if to be exact. It ran the length of the plate. Layer upon layer of rich creamy goodness. I could taste it. I salivated over it. I imagined myself being back at the party. I could hear the laughter, and then I imagined that The Architect felt the same happiness when he was designing. That was his piece of cake. That's the only sound he could hear, the sound of his hummingbird pencil. It certainly let him forget about Bruce, Wild Bill, and The

President of The Island. He needed his freedom from them all. I understood that. But I also realized that it should not hold up the dishing out their punishment. I understood that so clearly. So now I too could have my cake and eat it too.

CHAPTER 18.

Punishment Turned Up.

The meeting room had come back to order. Bruce was sat down by both Wild Bill and The President of The Island, who was aching to restart his story. He was a very important man, and his time at the podium had been little. Too little for such a man of massive self-importance, he thought. And he was right.

He was important. He was rich. And he was influential.

"I was a self-made man. I had cast my hand and it turned up aces, or so I thought." The President suddenly looked a little wobbly.

I had already researched The President of The Island. Where he lived. His family. His schooling. His mistresses. His indulgences. His club membership. His wine habits. And

I found that he was nothing more than a show-off. Although in another life, he could have been an architect.

You see, The President of The Island carefully built his life from a blueprint like an architect would. He worked hard and earned money, which became his foundation. Then he set his foundation in concrete. He poured more money into it and smoothed it over, reinforcing it exactly where he needed to. Next he erected walls with his business profile, and he covered the walls with his ability to be an invaluable resource, invaluable to his clients. Then he decorated the walls with his expertise, his contacts, his business acumen. He raised his roof based on the ballooning IT sector. He tiled his roof as a venture capitalist. And he put the icing on the cake by sending his children to the most exclusive schools to touch shoulders with the mega rich and the children of the mega influential. All in all his life was pretty rosy.

I asked myself how The President of The Island knew to insult The Architect. I then found out how he had heard of him in the very first instance. I found out The President had purchased the earliest house designed by the new genius of the architectural world: The Architect. The genius who straight out of university set the hounds barking with his unique take on architecture. Who brought everything down to the basics. Yes, The President bought an early house of The Architect. It was not opulent. Not modest. More seventies than eighties over-indulgence. More nineties suburban than eighties excess. It was not in the center of the city; it lay long and flat in the suburbs and was designed to encourage interaction with the family who lived there. It had a raised ceiling height. It had a flat roof. Local stone fascia. A long driveway that dissected the green grass like a motorway. It had glass. And class. And just the one camera.

When The President first insulted The Architect I decided to get gather information. I sent in my man under the false pretense to service the faulty electrical meter that connected the 240-vault supply from the street to his home. My man replaced the old model camera with a pencil-thin model, a camera that saw 360 degrees. And my eyes were truly opened.

I quickly realized that I had to attack The President from the bottom and unearth his foundations. Which was his money.

So what really happened at The Island was that I had my shit-shoot friend send in the rats again. But this time I let them stay. The next night I sent in more. And more the next night. And the next night. Then I sent them in to every bathroom in the building. It didn't matter if the exterminators took them away. I had thousands of rats standing by. It was rat heaven.

Then I called a friend who had a friend who was a journalist who needed money. I gave him the photos and the footage and the story about The Corporation being infested with rats, the story that showed that The Island was rat heaven.

The public health system closed The Corporation down. The Island was sinking. The venture capitalist, who was The President, started to lose his appeal in the market. His profile started to take a dive. The funds that fueled The Corporation slowed to a trickle. But the bills kept racing along. They kept heading the pack. They kept accumulating. The papers published photos of The President alongside the photos of the rats fucking. It made the cable news. It made the business section. It made international reports. The President was the poster boy, the poster boy of failure. It was his company after all. He thought he was the smartest guy in the room, but now he found himself in the anomalous position of being unable to pay for his own elevated living standard and that of his overly large establishment. So right now, with the doors locked, the Corporation had insufficient funds to service its debt obligations, and with that all of The President's credit cards were cancelled. As were those of his wife and his children. He lived on the never-never anyway like every other well-to-do president of a corporation.

He was not bankrupt—not yet. But the shame that he attracted was just as horrific. All of his current and future clients now knew about the rats and his less-than-stellar financial position. His banks had shut their doors. What money they had of his was frozen. And for the first time in his life, just like a normal, mortal man, he could not fill his expensive cars with petrol. He could not buy a loaf of bread. His children could not match the spending of their friends. And their friend's parents had alerted them to their friend's father's woes. While all this time more and more rats ran through his Corporation. Fucking. Shitting. Rooting around. Making headlines until I decided enough was enough.

The Corporation's foundations were weak. The icing on the cake had melted in the harsh sun of exposure. The roof The President tiled was fractured by the hammer of reality, created by the lack of funds. The ceiling he raised was smashed by him being identified as the failed pinup boy. The walls he decorated were smeared with the feces of his retreating connections. The walls he erected and covered crumbled with his falling profile.

Yes, I had The President of The Island on his knees.

The Architect was too busy to disturb with the news of The President's punishment. Especially me taking it to eight on the punishment scale. The Architect had a competition to win. And I had an office to run. We all knew that.

The Architect did ask one morning, after reading the business section of the newspaper, after seeing the headline on the front page of the same newspaper, after hearing about it on the radio news bulletin. He asked me if I knew anything about The President and The Island. I raised my chin and my lower lip. I made a pout. I made a sound that sounded like no. He looked and me and said, "Of course you don't." And with that he was gone.

Throughout the day I tried to gain his attention to tell him I did know something. But he was competing. He shooed me away.

Chapter 19.

I Lied to the Architect.

I did not tell The Architect the truth. I guess I lied. And I felt the emotion I normally do not. I felt guilt. It was a strange experience. It was situational. I was in a situation where I needed to lie to get myself out of trouble. Yes, I felt guilt. For some reason I could not live with myself after such a bare-faced lie. So I summoned The Architect to have it out with me. I demanded he hear me. He agreed after a verbal stoush.

Which is technically not true. In fact, I sent The Architect an e-mail to see if he had one minute in his busy design schedule. I never got a reply. In fact he left early that day; he took flight like a bird headed for the north in summer. So I took his position. I took one of his jackets. And I played both parts of the conversation I had to have with him. Mine and his.

Yes, I played both parts … The Architect and the Assistant. I explained to him, as the Assistant, that I needed to continue to punish The President of The Island so he would remember who he had denigrated.

I then put The Architect's jacket on and agreed with the Assistant. Agreed that the Assistant had done everything for the good of The Architect. And I agreed that the Assistant had not gone too far.

I then explained, as the Assistant, that I was not finished with The President of The Island. That I was not finished with Wild Bill. That I was not finished with Bruce.

I put The Architect's jacket on and supported the Assistant's actions, supported that whatever was going to take place was for the good of the firm and for the good of myself. I patted the Assistant on the back to show him support.

I took the jacket off to receive my pat on the back and realized quickly that it was quite hard to pat myself on the back while wearing one sleeve of The Architect's jacket, contorting my arm into such a position that I could feel the slap of pleasure. Quite hard indeed.

Then I put The Architect's jacket back on completely to smile at the Assistant and walk out of the room.

I returned after I took the jacket off and smiled to myself. And I started to create the new punishment sheet, the sheet that went all the way to eleven. Suddenly I felt less guilt. I closed The Architect's door on my way out of his office.

I stayed in my office all night. Watching the cameras. Replaying anything I thought would warrant putting my new punishment regime into practice. It's then that I remembered a saying. A saying that neither disturbed me nor made me smile, but I realized that it was true. The saying went: "Lies are simply tools we use to get us through the night."

It was then that I realized that there were many forms of lies: A big lie, based on information the victim already possesses. There was bluffing, based on the pretense of a capability one does not possess. There was a barefaced lie, directly spilled to those hearing it. A contextual lie, giving a false impression. There was being economical with the truth, like I was with The Architect. There was an emergency lie, when the truth may not be told; otherwise a third party would be harmed. There was lying by omission, when you leave out one important fact. There was a noble lie, assisting in keeping society orderly, and an exaggeration, or truth stretching.

You see, the psychology of lying started with Machiavellian intelligence, when at the age of four and a half children lie to avoid punishment for misdeeds. And there you have it with me. I lied to avoid punishment, and I added a sprinkle of pseudologia fantastica (habitual or compulsive) and mythomania (excessive or abnormal) lying, which brought me to the conclusion that I was indeed a liar. And a bloody good one. It also brought me to the conclusion that the less I told people, the less I had to lie.

CHAPTER 20.

The President Tells of the Domino Effect.

The President of The Island stood in front of the group and warranted to tell us everything. Everything, without a word of a lie.

As I studied him I could see that his face had dropped, like a small stroke had affected him. Not enough to disfigure him, just enough to afford a second glance. A person who suffered a stroke may recover, but survivors also suffered emotional changes, and that's the sort of stroke The President had. A stroke of the heart.

He stood in front of us a broken man with a dignity that had been washed and hung out to dry. He stood before us with nothing to lose because he had already lost it. Yes, he was going to tell us the truth and nothing but. The President started with an analogy, the domino effect; it was a common analogy to use. Let me explain.

In reality communism was the cause of the domino effect; in The President's case it was all about greed and money. So The President's money is communism in the analogy. The participants were China, Korea, Vietnam, Laos, Cambodia, Thailand, Malaysia, Indonesia, Burma, and India. In this case the very structures of The President's life. So in effect The President's life structures were the dominoes. The fighter for freedom and democracy was the United States. So The Architect's Assistant, that's me, was fighting for the cause, so I was the United States. The war waged was the Southeast Asia conflict. Or in this case, my war against the economical, strategic advantage The President held.

Stay with me here.

So The President's communism (greed) had lined up his dominoes (life) to wage his war against democracy (me). It was the job of the democracy fighter (me) to bring the world back to balance (and punish The Corporation).

So I borrowed a theory from US president Dwight D. Eisenhower. "You have a row of dominoes set up; you knock over the first one, and what will happen to the last one is the certainty that it will go over very quickly."

I had knocked over all of The President's dominoes with my rats. Now I had the fallen dominoes right in the palm of my hand. So I restacked them in my own order to see how The President of the Island would react.

I kept the foundation domino firmly in my hand while I put his icing on the cake—the kids—on the very bottom of the stack. Yes, the squishy icing of the cake that was the kids on the bottom. I laid the feeble walls on top of them. The slippery profile would not stay in place; every time someone walked past it and leaned on it, it slipped. The invaluable resource and expertise that shored up The President's walls had been stolen. The IT business still had legs; it's just that

The President had no software, no systems, no hardware to run his business. It was frozen. Frozen on his island.

The kids were feeling the pressure of being on the bottom. They were trying to shoulder the acrimonious gossip about their father. They kept it all together, until one day when the pressure of being on the bottom seriously hurt the kids. So they lashed out verbally at their father.

This cut The President to the core. You see, The President could handle what other people thought of him. But it was his own personal opinion of himself that hurt him the most. And when his own kids questioned him. He was shattered.

And all because I had taken away the one thing that made him happy. His money. I took away the money that made him different. That made him powerful. That made him secure. And now it was gone.

After I had tipped over the first domino, I knew the rest was history.

The newspaper loved it. I loved it. But what amazed me most was the amount of people who craved to see the rich fall from glory. The richer the better. The further the fall, the better.

The President stood in front of us and explained it had taken seventy-eight days to rid The Island of the rats. "If only the Pied Piper had been around," he said with a half smile. And with the reopening of The Corporation's doors The President restarted his business machine. But alas, his clients had already departed. They had already taken up with his competition who stayed in business. The competition who stayed out of the Headlines. The competition who kept their reputation.

The President had to lay off staff, to reduce his costs, to refinance, to try to recoup his losses. It was a sad day, the day he handed back his mortgage papers to the bank. But not before he came back to see The Architect one last time. The

President walked in to The Architect's office unannounced. The Architect graced him with his presence. There was little small talk. The two did not have much in common. The President explained that he was selling his home, the home The Architect had designed. He explained that if he had a signed document stating that it was in fact the very first home designed by The Architect it would garner him additional dollars. Additional dollars to get him by. And with that The Architect walked out of the meeting.

Later that day The Architect approached me with an addressed envelope. He handed it to me and left. I steamed it open and saw to my amazement that The Architect had indeed produced the document for The President. I was shocked. I could not let The Architect go through with it and sell himself. So I destroyed it.

The President broke down in tears in front of the group as he told his story. He wept. And shook. And swayed. Fluid poured from his body like a punctured waterbed. His nose was a tap. His eyes ran like a stream. He let the tears run down his face. He never wiped them away. The salt stained his cheeks, leaving marks like a native warrior, scarred to show the feats he had endured to become a man.

Yes, The President was indeed scarred. The day he became that man, The President man, he was scarred. And it was only now the sting of initiation was paining him.

Wild Bill stood next to The President and man cuddled him, but not in a gay way. He feebly put his arm around him, his outstretched arm locked in the uncomfortable pattern of insincerity. Wild Bill leaned his head over until it rested. Not on The President's shoulder. But on his own shoulder.

Both men stood there for a long time. Until finally The President shuffled out of the man hug and sat himself on the chair. To sit, heavy with defeat while Wild Bill stood oddly. Centre stage without a word to say.

Chapter 21.

A Frozen Frame.

While the gang in the room composed themselves. Wiped their noses. Tucked their shirts in. Took a piss. Let me tell you a little more about Trophy and her first sitting with the Artist. She always brings out the best in a man, I say, the inner animal lust in a man.

The Artist, like Wild Bill, had a lust for animalism. Only his animals had claws and tails and heads. They came in a frozen state, in a truck. As you know the Artist hijacked Wild Bill's cool room. He changed the cool room to freezing temperature and stacked his animals one by one.

The Artist's ark was a small, specialized version of Noah's ark. A moose. A dog as big as a horse. A prairie fox. A cougar. They had all been freshly killed and then were snap frozen like a prawn, insides intact. It was all part of the Artist's plan. He freed them from their frozen state just long enough to manhandle their position. Then he set them back to freeze. Perfectly in pose.

The Artist laid his mottled canvas drop cloth on the floor of the dungeon. He set the temperature at seventeen degrees Celsius. And he sat in anticipation. Waiting for his subjects to thaw out a little.

Finally, after an hour or so. Sixty-eight minutes, to be exact—of waiting by the Artist and his slightly thawed animal, his real subject entered the room.

Trophy looked uncomfortable. Her arms clung to her dressing gown like a spider to its web. The dressing gown momentarily moved about her body. But it never moved very far.

So the Artist made her a cup of herbal tea. It was in fact rice tea. It warmed her body and her confidence. She drank it slowly until her cup was empty. Then the Artist poured her a refill, which delayed the inevitable. She drank this cup more slowly. And then she had to go to the bathroom. When she returned the Artist had repositioned the frozen moose. It stood on its hind legs. Head reared to the sky, its mouth open, its tongue flapping. The moose's frozen groin stuck out proud. The Artist gently moved Trophy to arch herself between the moose's hind legs. He positioned her hands so they firmed the ground. He asked her to raise her bottom so it just touched the frozen moose's crotch.

The cold fur sent shivers through Trophy's body. She shook a little, forgetting where she was, forgetting what she was doing. The discomfort of the cold made her nipples involuntarily erect. And at just that moment the Artist took a shot on his trusty Canon 5D. It showed Trophy in the perfect, vulnerable position. And with that the Artist said she was done.

Trophy sat and had another rice tea watching the Artist reform the thawing moose into a new position before putting it back into the freezer. Then he carried over the prairie fox and stood it frozen on his canvas. Trophy voluntarily left her tea and made her way to the canvas, dropping her robe to reveal her youthfulness. Her taught skin. Her twenty-eight-year-old body. The Artist laid her on her back. Her legs open. Her head pushed as far back as possible. He tousled her hair. He picked up his camera and then asked her to push her crotch into the frozen prairie fox's mouth. The instant chill had the same effect as before, making Trophy writhe against the sudden cold. And with that he released her. He repeated positions with the dog that was as big as a horse. He had the animal lie on its back while Trophy sat over it. The Cougar, with its tongue extended, close enough to lick Trophy's nipple. He refroze the cougar and had Trophy lie lengthwise against its torso. He refroze the moose and had her ride it. He refroze the dog and had her kiss it. And everything was just one quick shot. With that he thanked Trophy. She lingered a second before leaving and walked away slowly. She heard his dungeon door close behind her and the lock set in place.

From that day on no one saw the Artist until one hour exactly before mealtimes when he would leave his space, padlock his dungeon, and head to rattle the pans.

Breakfast was a warm compote of fruit alongside a goat cheese omelet. Goose eggs with a splash of Tabasco, and crispy pancetta. Lunch was caramelized fennel, asparagus, duck egg, walnuts, and muscatels. Dinner was grilled suckling pig, french potatoes, and warm applesauce. Grilled pork torta with cabbage, coriander, and mayo. And with every meal was Wild Bill's special drink, handmade by the Artist himself.

The Artist always started the meal by saying how great, young, and revitalized Wild Bill looked. He espoused that it must be his special drink, and then he went quiet. The conversation quickly turned to painting. The upcoming exhibition. Questions about how the painting process was going. Prices. Catalogues. Guest lists. But the only person talking was Wild Bill. The other two ate quietly.

Directly after dinner the Artist bunkered down in his dungeon, his lair, only to come out next meal to cook and eat and then return to his painting.

A month passed.

One day after breakfast he cleared the plates and lingered. Lingered and made rice tea. Wild Bill returned from his home office and rinsed his glass of the remains of the Artist's drink. It was then that it hit him.

"You've finished?"

"Yes."

"Then show me. Show me now. I insist. And tell me what you titled them."

The Artist explained that he was not a noted writer. He explained that his paintings were his words. But as agreed for this exhibition the Artist had titled each one; yes, for the very first time he had titled each piece for the catalogue. The artist pulled a piece of paper from his pocket. He had scribbled long and small sentences above and below each other. Wild Bill grabbed the paper and started reading the smudged writing.

"Nipple coated in cougar spittle."

"Lip sprinkled with sperm."

"Finger coated in animal chocolate."

"Vagina with hot dog, mustard, and relish."

Wild Bill threw the note on the ground. Standing. Indignant. Red-faced and bellowed for Trophy: "*Trophy. Trophy. Trophy.*"

Wild Bill was red. He paced on the spot. His thousand dollar shoes scuffing the terrazzo tiles. He huffed and puffed. He called out again. This time louder.

"*Trophy!*"

Trophy walked down the steps as if in slow motion. Her

open-fronted Prada jacket fell off her body like molting hair, her coat of confidence worn high on her smile. Her mid-waist skirt fell like falling powder snow. Light as it was. It was sky blue. Trophy wore a seventies-inspired top. A boob tube of sorts. She walked on four-inch heels. Strappy. Revealing. Showing off her painted toes.

"You screamed for me. Well, I am here now."

Wild Bill looked beaten, just for one second. Then he turned to the Artist.

"Don't say a fucking thing. Show me the paintings now. Show me now. Then we can all discuss the titles. The titles that already draw tears from my eyes. But not mine alone. I will attest to that."

The artist searched for the key in his pocket. Then he unbolted the lock and threw open the dungeon doors. Although it was his house Wild Bill was startled by the space. Even if it was just in his mind. In his imagination. As if magic happened in here.

The flood of light blinded them as the Artist pulled back the doors that shut out the world outside the dungeon. The air was thick with the particles of space. The particles that together formed a formidable shadow against the streams of light. The particles that moved to clear the air so the Artist's paintings were revealed.

And with that Wild Bill set his eyes on the twenty-eight paintings. He dropped his head to his hands, scooping it at shoulder height. He wept. He raised his head to look back at the paintings. Then he dropped his head again. He continued to weep. He dropped to his knees. His elbows touched the dungeon floor. His head followed. As did the tears.

Trophy stood and stared, her stare getting the better of her. She shuffled small steps. Closer. Closer to the paintings. She looked at her own form, or what there was to make out. She traced her finger one inch above the thick, buckled streams of paint. The streams that seemed to run for miles. The streams that seemed to tell a story of their own. The streams that were connected to her form. Trophy walked closer to each painting and repeated the finger thing just one inch from the actual paint. Then she returned to her starting position. And stood still and silent.

Wild Bill spun around on his haunches, his shirt collecting the loose dirt from the dungeon floor, and he grabbed the Artist's ankles. Grabbed his legs. And he cried openly on the Artist's jeans.

All three stayed like that for a very long time, all three connected by the Artist's paintings.

Let me paint the picture for you. A picture of the paintings. The Artist's canvas was his creative mind. The Artist himself was the vampire. Trophy was the blood. Trophy's blood flowed through the Artist until he sucked her life energy. The rest was now history. You see, there was not one body part of Trophy in any painting. Not one discernible limb. Breast. Leg. Torso. Nipple. Each and every painting was an abstract of abstract proportions. What everyone did see was the passion. The verve. The pathos. The emotion. Wild Bill was feeling it now.

The Artist helped Wild Bill to his feet, carrying him outside the dungeon.

The kitchen table was cleared of floral arrangements while the Artist laid Wild Bill down. Wild Bill was breathing heavily. Gulping air. Trying to swallow the emotion in the room. Eventually Wild Bill could sit up. He stared for a very, very long time and then opened his mouth.

The Artist handed him a glass of his special Wild Bill concoction. Wild Bill gulped before he could speak. "The animalism. It's … It's … mesmerizing. I thought I was Trophy's animal."

The Artist took a deep breath. "Trophy. Could you please leave us?" She obliged.

The Artist turned to Wild Bill. "You are her animal. You just need to remind her." And with that Wild Bill again cuddled the Artist. "You see, man is the only creature that consumes without producing. Man does not give milk, does not lay eggs, cannot pull a plough or run fast enough to catch rabbits. Yet he is lord of the animals. He sets them to work. For himself."

And with that Wild Bill again burst into tears.

CHAPTER 22.

A Present from Wild Bill.

Wild Bill stood before the group, uncomfortable. We could all tell that the next part of his story was weighing heavily on him. So let me take over and explain "the gift."

Wild Bill went shopping for a present, but not your ordinary present—not a handbag, not a car, not a diamond. Trophy had all of those. This present was as much for Wild Bill as it was for Trophy. For if he was to be lord of the animals. He must be lord of Trophy.

With the smell of success in his nose, Wild Bill appointed himself to the premier perfumery to buy nothing but agar. Yes, agar.

You may never have heard of this secret, but agar was an ancient scent known for its aphrodisiac properties. It was a true gift to the world. And was in most cases paired with saffron, rose, wood, or spice. But Wild Bill wanted agar in its hard-core offering, paired with nothing but Mysore sandalwood.

Wild Bill knew he would again fall in love today, and not just with the scent. He would fall in love with the intrigue around agar as much as agar itself. He hoped Trophy would also fall in love with the sticky resinous substance from Aquilaria trees in Southeast Asia.

Wild Bill sat and listened to the perfumer tell his loved story of the distillers who took agar to market in Bombay and Bangkok just as their ancient masters did, with secrecy and adulteration to rival the opium trade.

Its rareness and price made this perfume perfect for what he had in mind. The perfumer called it "the new black," and Wild Bill asked to smell it raw. As soon as it entered his nostrils Wild Bill was indeed in love. With one sniff Wild Bill was effusing with words like dirty. Feral. Brutish. Animal. Wood. Smoke. Dark. Complex. This was just the beast Wild Bill wanted—Wild Bill's new black. He asked if black was dangerous.

The perfumer assured that him in the right hands it was not. He told Wild Bill of agar's modern history, how it was introduced to the mass market via select clients and how it took everyone by surprise. How intoxicated people became. They had to be introduced to it slowly, like a strong drug.

Wild Bill heard how Tom Ford introduced it to great success. Then within several years houses like Guerlain, Dior, and Caron all released agar scents. Niche houses like Juliette Has a Gun, Le Labo, Bond, Armani Prive, Bryedo, and Kilian all brought out the lighter, gentler side to agar. But that was not for Wild Bill. He demanded the most pure agar he could afford. And he could afford a lot.

This was to be a treat indeed, a treat for Trophy, a sorry card to be played for forgiveness. Plus it was for Wild Bill after all. Wild Bill had not been feeling himself. He felt well—very well—lighter, not leaner, but not bloated. However his normal animalistic sexual drive had been on hold. It sat delicately underneath his skin where in the past it was on show for all to see, oozing out of every pore, dancing on his skin with his perspiration. But not at the moment. He questioned his age, his fitness, his lust for Trophy and came up with the only answer a man needed. He needed a date with Trophy and the agar. And with that, it was arranged.

All three of the household ate dinner as usual. The Artist cooked a Greek feast. They dined on fried school prawns, crisp and salty, tossed in fish sauce and drizzled with honey, scattered with almonds; smoky grilled pita bread; horiatiki salad with creamy barrel-aged feta. But the star of the meal was the Skaras, slow braised lamb shoulder resting on succulent green beans and lemon potatoes. The meal was exquisite. Wild Bill drank his potion after the meal, and everyone left the Artist to clean away by himself. Wild Bill and Trophy returned to the eagle's nest.

The door was closed. Locked. The lights were dimmed. Trophy left to dress in something more feminine. When she returned Wild Bill was sitting on the bed, hands behind his back, like a small child with a secret. Trophy lit up.

"A present for me?"

"I'm sorry for not being myself lately."

"I know you are. So what is it?"

"It's the new black. Everyone is saying it. It's the new black, the new black. Remember that from today it has to be black."

Trophy looked at the wrapping paper. It was not what even she was used to seeing. The paper that held the surprise was antique, handmade from worn-out sails, softened by wind and rain, bleached by the sun to a soft white. The ribbon holding the secret featured a vintage passementerie from France. Trophy unfolded the ribbon without damage, rubbing it across her hand and then her cheek. She unfolded the paper that had sailed across the world ten times. She held it up to the light, letting it fall across her face, covering her forehead to her chin. She inhaled the paper, the salt, the history. The paper crept into her nose, sealing her passages so she had to breathe through her mouth; the paper rose and fell with her breath. Like a small child playing with the paper that wrapped the gift, Trophy was enthralled, and all the time Wild Bill watched her. In anticipation.

The antique paper found its way to the bed. Perfect. Straight. Hardly creased. It lay alongside the perfect ribbon.

Now it was the box's turn to flip open—the box that cradled the agar. The box was soft and sensual. The bottle was simple, frosted, made in Lalique Crystal. Each "flacon" holding the Agar was a precious limited edition, numbered and signed. But it was the dark brooding agar that held Wild Bill's breath.

Trophy gently moved the stopper from side to side to free the viscous liquid. The seal was tight. It moved slowly until it popped like a small champagne cork and the flood of perfume filled the room. Trophy felt dizzy. She tried to hold her head back away from the addictive agar, but it was not to be. As Trophy tried to refit the stopper Wild Bill could no longer contain himself. He lunged at Trophy, jolting her hand so the prized agar surged from the bottle, splashing it so it wet her see-through top with a huge dollop. The gooey agar clung to Trophy's cleavage. And within a flash Wild Bill was atop her.

Wild Bill pawed Trophy. Pawed her top and everything underneath it. He grappled her like a wrestling coach teaching a novice. His hands were perfectly placed; hers were floundering in midair. His head was perfectly positioned for maximum effect; hers hung limply. The stunned glaze in her eyes was either from the agar or from the animal pawing her.

To say Wild Bill was taking his time was a mistake. He was rushing like he had never rushed before.

Trophy stayed clothed. It was just the way she wore her clothes that would have startled even her, had she had the luxury to view the footage. Bits were too high. Bits were too low. Rounds of body were exposed. Others were smothered in fabric.

And just as Wild Bill was ready to do the deed, he lost his will. Or his will lost him. His face was red raw, his breathing short and fast, but his will was not up to it. All the talking in the world would not get it up. You see, Wild Bill liked dirty talk in the bedroom. So he started to reprimand "it". He spoke like the devil to it, but it did not even quiver. He grabbed it like a soft doll, but it did little more than project itself like a squeezed pork sausage. So he yelled at Trophy to talk to it. Trophy grabbed it in her fingertips and spoke softly to it, so softly it went further to sleep. So she shook it up a bit. It did little more than stay in her hand and started to redden. So she grabbed the world-famous agar and dabbed a good drip onto the eye of it.

Wild Bill leaped off the bed and started yelping. The agar had penetrated his skin. And what neither of them knew was that Wild Bill was allergic to perfume fixatives.

Wild Bill held it stinging in his hand as he looked back at Trophy and growled with his teeth bared, between yelps, with his face contorted. Then he left the eagle's nest. Doing up his fly. Cursing. And yelping.

Trophy pulled her clothes back into place. Straightening them. Pulling them up. Pulling them down. Then she noticed her perfect antique wrapping paper and antique ribbon. Crushed. Crumpled. Torn. Destroyed.

Trophy looked at the door Wild Bill walked out of and screamed.

Chapter 23.

It Comes with an Instruction Manual.

A week had passed since the eagle's nest disaster. Sex had already become a thing of the past in the weeks leading up to the agar calamity, so the last week was more of a normal state between Wild Bill and Trophy, two consenting adults without any mutual consent.

They passed each other in the bathroom. In the shower. Each tried not to look at the other in a compromising situation. Pissing. During bodily functions. Eating. Walking down the same corridor.

It had gotten to Wild Bill far more than it got to Trophy. So just before bed he openly apologized again, and begged for forgiveness, although not once did he comment on his inability to perform sexually. Nor did he specifically bring up the agar sting on his penis. But he did enough to be awarded the opportunity to kiss Trophy on the cheek. A cheek that was shown in all its glory, covered in night cream. And with a smile on his face he kissed that cheek and went to sleep.

The next day they were more cordial with each other, still making certain they did not step on each other's toes.

They were too busy tiptoeing around each other to enjoy their wonderful house. Their eagle's nest. Their houseguest. Too busy to luxuriate on the upcoming art gallery opening. Too busy to think of good things. Comfortable things. Warm things. They were definitely too sour and on edge to appreciate happiness.

The time now for Wild Bill was all about recreating that equilibrium of marriage. Serenity. Unity. Knowing. And until that was done. Nothing could be appreciated.

Wild Bill worked out badly in his gym, injuring himself as his concentration left him, as he forget what task he was doing. He ate breakfast and drank his special brew. But no one spoke. The artist was busily sketching. Trophy was busily brewing. Wild Bill was busy sweating on his ability to resolve his disconnect with Trophy.

As Wild Bill got up and went to leave the house The Architect built, he stopped and waited for Trophy to notice him. Wild Bill waited—something he was not used to. Trophy looked up without stopping to chew. Wild Bill spoke softly, almost apologizing.

"I have a surprise for you."

Trophy looked hard at his face. Wild Bill half smiled.

"A present. I'll give it to you later today."

And with that Trophy dropped her eyes.

I was watching the cameras live as the drama happened. So I rewound it and played it back. Rewound it and played it back. A smile broke out on my face involuntarily. I spewed forth: "Indeed he has a present for you, Trophy. Indeed."

Trophy went about her day as usual until the buzzer at the gate rang. She pressed the controller and let the courier commence his journey up the long driveway, past the formal classic planting of the garden, past the prized American contemporary sculptures featuring four distinct mixed-metal pieces. The first sculpture form was a rising of undulating spears, abstract spears pushing up into the sky, aggressive in their form, strong in their number. The spears soared high above the large-scale orb that sat heavy on the ground, made from rusted barbed wire, steel ribbons, bearings, and motor parts, which led the courier past the massive quill that seemed to float and bend in the breeze, its rusted form tapering to a needle point, sixty feet into the heavens. It led him past the whimsy that was not a car, not a buggy, not a scooter, not a tractor. But was a bit of all of them. The flames roared out of the rear of the vehicle in bright red and yellow steel rods. The rear wheels sat huge, the front wheels tiny. The metal balls that held the front low to the ground were like cannon balls. The frame was a piece of fluid marvel. Everything was in stainless steel, weathering steel, and bronze plate.

But the courier I'm sure was oblivious to any of it. His job was to make the delivery. And that's what he did.

Trophy held the present. Yes, she knew it was her present, firmly in her palms. It was light but boxy—oblong to be exact. Trophy tossed it lightly and then decided not to throw it around too much in case it was fragile. She paused and looked toward the Artist's dungeon for too long before she went upstairs to see what Wild Bill had sent her.

Unwrapping the parcel was a chore. There was an outside wrapper and an inside wrapper. There was a note between the sheets of paper, a small typed note. Trophy lifted it. It was a love poem of sorts, an erotic love poem, an instruction sheet more like it. It had specifics and procedure written out. And it was sealed with a kiss.

Trophy separated the inside paper and sat looking at her present. She was not shocked. Not really. She stood and walked around the room looking back at it. Thinking. Thinking. Questioning herself. Then she looked at it no more. She picked it up and sat it next to her underwear and shut the drawer. She took the note, looked at her watch, and went to the gym.

When Trophy returned she had purpose on her face. She reread the love poem. It was titled "The Wolves." It read like most poems written in lust. It had a start, a middle, and an end. But it was the bits around those bits that were the real message. If she dissected it, she would see that it could have been written by a sixteen-year-old boy or a boy about to have sex for the very first time, a boy asking the question and hoping for the answer. But no. It was obviously written by Wild Bill—but a new Wild Bill; one who was a little unsure of himself, and this was his way of getting all that surety back.

Wild Bill came home exactly the same time every day at 6:15.

Trophy looked at her watch and went to work like a machine.

It was just 5:00 p.m. already. Trophy showered. Shaved under her arms. Made certain she was tidy everywhere else. She dried herself and played with her hair for fifteen minutes, getting out the blow dryer and folding under the ends that sat just below her shoulder. She looked at herself in the mirror, turning sideways to check that she had not put on weight, to check that there was no cellulite. Then she opened her underwear drawer to pick one of Wild Bill's favorites. And there it was staring her in the face. Her present. She gently moved it aside as she took out multiple sets of underwear. Deciding on a baby-doll top. It was see-through. Sheer. And stunning. Just the sort they wear in high-class love scenes on film. And that was all she chose.

Trophy looked at her watch. It was five past six. She

had ten minutes to kill. So she washed her present. Patted it dry. And sat it on the bed. Trophy reread the poem and laid the pillows just as it directed. She lowered the lights and placed herself—the poem said to drape herself on the bed—in exactly the position the poem said. At exactly 6:14, Trophy picked up her present and did as the note asked.

You see, Trophy had been sent a black jelly. Yes, a black jelly. Exactly like the one The Architect had made famous. And with that black jelly Trophy did everything the poem had stated. Specifically remembering at this exact time what Wild Bill had said days before. It had to be black.

Wild Bill walked into the eagle's nest at exactly 6:15. Trophy did not stop to welcome him home. No. The poem had stated she must perform as if he was not there. She was to let him walk around the room. Record it if he wanted. She was not to stop until she orgasmed. Then Wild Bill could join her on the bed. Or not. Even though she was in control of the black jelly, Wild Bill was in control of the situation.

When Wild Bill walked in he was shocked. Startled. Had he caught Trophy doing what she did when he was away? But she was not stopping. She was not afraid for him to see her use the black jelly? Had he caught her putting on a show for him? Was this her way of saying everything was forgiven?

Wild Bill did indeed walk around the bed, watching Trophy. He sat near her and moved closer to her crotch to watch the black jelly at work. Then he backed away and blushed.

He moved in to kiss Trophy and stop her. But his kiss did not stop her rhythm.

Wild Bill stood at the end of the bed watching, comfortably uncomfortable.

He put his hand inside his pocket and took out a small gift-wrapped box, laying it on the end of the end. Then he left. Trophy had not seen or heard him leave. She was almost at the end of her show. And within another minute she was done. Her cheeks were ruddy. Her blood pressure had risen considerably. She felt warm all over. And content.

Trophy opened her eyes and looked for Wild Bill. But he was gone. She imagined him in the bathroom getting ready to join her so she rolled over and lay prostrate for a while longer. Bill never appeared. She raised herself onto one elbow and saw the box. Trophy moved the black jelly and inched down toward it, flicking the bow off it with precision. Opening the box she found a bangle. A beautiful rose gold antique bangle from Italy, solid, Sicilian, with bold links in 585 (14 kt) gold weighing 17.55 grams. Off it hung a classic Sicilian Trinacria–designed pendant handmade by a goldsmith of merit. Trophy put it on and reread the poem sent with her black jelly. It said she was to pretend nothing had even happened. Not to talk to Wild Bill about it. So she showered and dressed and walked down to dinner.

The Artist had prepared another great meal. A spring-broad bean, mozzarella, and snow pea salad. Grilled sardines, coated in fresh lemon juice and extra virgin olive oil. Followed by three individual slow-cooked organic eggs wrapped in crisp brick pastry, served with rich potato cream, Spanish ham, and micro cress. And tonight they all ate and spoke to each other as if it were their duty more than their want.

When Wild Bill told this to the group he could see everyone moving quietly in their seats. Bruce was definitely embarrassed. The President didn't know where to look. But I was kind of excited. I would have loved Wild Bill to go into more detail about the show Trophy put on, but it was not to be. Wild Bill asked for an adjournment to calm himself down. Which is what we got. Although everyone knew that the night was still far from over.

CHAPTER 24.

The Architect's Old Drug.

At work The Architect had found his old drug. An old favorite. Hidden deep within himself. He thought he had lost the desire, but it was good to see it was back. It was evident that he needed his drug to function. He realized that stopping the drug had given him real withdrawal symptoms.

It was both a physical and a mental dependence. It was his pain relief, his drug to dispel anxiety, to dissolve away peer pressure. It was his secret weapon against depression.

The Architect had grown up in an environment of illicit drug use. He watched his parents using. Then even as a child he experimented himself, falling deeper and deeper under the same spell.

He himself had access to the drug every day. He lived in a culture that accepted such drug use. It's all they did.

He was addicted to something other than opiates. Other

than narcotics. Other than amphetamines. Other than cocaine. Other than alcohol. Other than barbiturates. Other than LSD. Other than cannabis. But he displayed all the same symptoms of dependence.

The Architect displayed continued use even when his health and family suffered. He did not take part in outside activities because of his drug. Did not socialize. He was secretive about his drug use and used his drug even when alone. Especially when he was alone.

The Architect had experienced withdrawal before. And it was only now that he realized he was again dependent. Totally dependent, even though he hid it well. It did not show up when he had his medical check-up. It did not screen in his urine or his blood, and so he was not sent to rehabilitation.

The Architect realized that there was no cure for his drug abuse. He had tried to deny it before. But it was the bi-annual architects' competition that brought back the hunger for his drug. Plus he had found the perfect place to shoot up. It was the basement under The Architect's office. It was cooler than the office above. The Architect did not like to sweat. It was quieter. He liked quiet. There were little or no interruptions. Interruptions only to urinate. To eat. To quench his thirst. The rest of the time his drug controlled him, kept him manic and calm at the same time. His mind felt awake on his drug. He felt invincible on his drug. Untouchable. He knew he had to have doses of it to stay sane. So sane he stayed.

Yes, The Architect had again discovered his love of architecture, his drug for life. And with his drug he drew. Designed. Invented. Imagined. His drug was his work.

I kept the daily chore of the office from him. I rehearsed and learned to mimic his voice. Clients did not know if they were speaking to The Architect or his Assistant. I even started to dress like him. I changed my hair, dyed it, had it re-styled. I started to wear his old jackets, the ones The Architect left in the office cupboard. They fit me like a glove. Then I slowly changed my shirts, trousers, shoes. I changed them all slowly so The Architect did not even notice. I wore fake reading glasses to match his look. I often startled myself passing a window. I was becoming him. For all the right reasons.

The Architect's productivity increased on his drug. His output was nothing short of amazing. His imagination was his only limit. His risk taking was enormous. And I became his site manager. I worked the schedules. Worked the trades. I became the link between The Architect's vision and the final masterpiece standing. I became the conduit. The facilitator. The technical go-to guy. While The Architect was happy to sit away from the world, alone, at a cool eighteen degrees, on his drug.

The Architect did not even visit the final buildings when they were built, did not see them in person. For he always imagined them perfect, and that vision stayed with him.

As I received the cold hard designs on the cold hard paper, I could have put them straight in the bin. I could have substituted my own designs for his. He would never have known. The clients would never have known. He never left his basement to read the architectural tabloids, the blogs— never. I could fuck his works of art up if I had wanted. But I never did. There was something inside me that I heard calling out every day, softly calling out, that one day I was to be the real Architect. Yes, one day I was to be the real hero. And soon enough everyone would know it. But to achieve it I had to stay strong. And patient. And work hard.

Chapter 25.

The Group Is Ready to Continue.

It was now dark in the room where we all sat, hot, stuffy. The air was heavy with guilt, shame, remorse, helplessness. A small light shone on Bruce, in a small circle above him. It exposed the beads of perspiration on his forehead, on his lip, under his beard.

Bruce stood in the center of the circle. No one fought him for his place. No one tried to pull him aside. He was left center stage.

I knew this part of his story was coming. I just wanted to hear it from Bruce's own mouth and see what he was prepared to tell us.

Bruce explained that after the fright of me explaining his guest accommodation, Placenta Haven, he returned home after a couple of days living in the wild. He had comfortably reentered his house on weekends and resumed his life. Everything seemed normal until the weekend he drove four hours to his stunning house and found it sitting on the ground like a giant shoebox, covered by a red splattered flapping sheet. Only the flapping sheets had been tied down to the sides. I had wrapped a giant bow around it and left a bottle of sparkling wine on the doorstep. I knew from Bruce's party that he did not appreciate champagne.

Bruce saw his guest accommodation with disbelief. Then he read the nameplate: Placenta Haven, which was written in Helvetica bold, simple but strong. You see, I had the builder erect a solid timber plaque and hang the name over the front door of his guest accommodation. It was then, upon seeing it, upon reading it, that Bruce again ran for the hills. Screaming. And this time he had no intention of ever coming back.

Bruce explained that the very first nightfall was the start of his newfound life. The start of his new friendship. You see, the fox that sat on the hill watching us party had not gone very far. This part of the desert was his. The hill was his. He found Bruce the very first evening. He realized that Bruce was not a threat. He realized that he was lost. A lost soul. So the fox let Bruce follow him.

The very first evening, and every evening after, the fox stood on the hilltop, legs planted, claws digging into the raw earth, holding his position against the wind while it buffeted his fur, sniffing the sky, smelling the colors turn from blue to pink to orange and then purple. The fox looked as if he were controlling the color change. Smelling them from one to the next. His nose was pointed high into the sky until everything had turned to a purple black. The blackness was the alarm that sent the fox on its way like a clock chiming. Bruce mimicked him perfectly. Standing near to the fox while the wind buffeted his hair. His head raised, smelling in the night. Racing off after the fox as it fled.

The fox was methodical in its path. He was quick. He did

not divert. Bruce had to work extra hard to keep up. Every now and then the fox smelled the air and stopped. Stopped until Bruce could see him. Then he moved off. For the kill.

Bruce watched as the methodical fox tracked his prey. He looked for snakes, mice, rabbits fowl, rats. Foxes are actually omnivores, you know. They eat things besides meat. They eat grasshoppers, beetles, insects, berries, corn, nuts, grasses. The fox stalked his prey, getting close enough to run it down.

You see, the fox actually kills its prey by cutting off its airway. So if the prey did not die of a heart attack after being caught, it would die a slow death. There would be no blood, no drip trail to follow, no ferocious dismembering of its prey.

The fox was also a master teacher. He would bring home live prey to teach the young how to kill. But he was a loner.

Foxes live alone, single, until mating season. Then they again flee to hunt alone and live alone until next they mate. The fox was a lot like Bruce, not that he had ever mated.

This first night, and forever after, Bruce followed the fox and watched it sneak closer to its prey, upwind, seeing in the dark, assessing where the prey could escape, mentally cutting off the escape channel, saving its own breath, its energy until the last moment—the very last moment—ready for the attack.

Bruce watched the fox smell the rat. The fox smelled the rat's sniffing nose, its darting eyes; smelled its beating heart. And just when the rat least expected it, the fox struck. The rat ran, darted for cover, for freedom. The fox circled, its head always forward, its body bending at ninety-degree angles. The fox's feet scratched the earth as the only trace of the scuffle that was taking place. And just like that the fox had the rat in its mouth. The teeth did not pierce the rat's skin, did not leave a trail of blood. The rat fell limp. It was playing dead, or it had died of fright. The fox stopped and smelled the air, looking in Bruce's direction. It walked toward Bruce, leaving the rat meters from his feet, as if Bruce was to instinctively know what to do next. The rat lay on the desert floor, still, and then suddenly, like Lazarus, it sprang to life and ran off. The fox started to chase, but the race was lost. The fox stopped to look at Bruce.

Bruce dropped his head for a second, and the fox was gone. When he looked up Bruce smelled the air and felt the coming cold. Felt the need for shelter. A hide. A place to stay out of the weather. A place to sleep. Bruce had found an old hollow log close to where the fox slept. He lay down inside it and fell asleep. When he woke to the sound of the fox baying at the moon, Bruce felt the corpse of a dead rat under his face. The fox stuttered in his baying, not looking back but smelling the air as he realized that Bruce was awake. Bruce fumbled in his pockets and found his safety matches, which he always carried in case his stunning low-slung home ever lost power. Soon there was a fire roasting the small desert rat. Bruce and the fox could smell the taste of it. Bruce salivated as he pulled the creature from over the flame. Pulling its limbs apart like a surgeon. Without his knowing it, the fox had sat himself down near the fire. Not too close. Just far enough away to make a beeline if Bruce turned feral. Bruce stopped and looked at the rat, deciding whether to share his dinner. He was hungry. But the fox had done the real work. So Bruce decided that for half of what little food he was about to receive, he was grateful.

After they had both eaten Bruce curled up like the fox. Mimicking it. Bruce saw in the fox a kindred spirit. Dirty. Brown. Black. A free spirit. A spirit not confined by convention. Not needing of anything more than shelter from the elements. Bruce decided that tomorrow he would dig a home in the hillside near the fox. Near his kindred spirit.

The morning came quickly, too quickly for Bruce. The

night had been long. And dark. And Bruce did not want it to end. Daylight brought him the reality of his normal world. For Bruce the darkest hour had just begun. And it was going to last all day, as the daylight hurt Bruce's eyes.

Bruce, like the fox, tried to sleep all day, so he could run after the fox and hunt all night. His vision at night improved. It was not normal for a human to have good night vision. But Bruce's improbably large and bulging eyeballs, his misshapen and enormous optical aperture, or pupil, made him a giant at seeing with a very small quantity of light. Bruce's spectrum range was not great. But he had a chemical inside him that made him see in the dark. It was rhodopsin, even though it could have been the clear night skies, the radiant starlight, or the moonlight that helped Bruce. Whatever it was, Bruce was an animal in the dark.

Bruce told the group assembled before him how he had been living like a fox in the desert for about a month before The Architect asked the Assistant to see the last week of tapes.

Startled by the request, and even more startled by the fact that this was The Architect's first venture from his basement, I, the Assistant immediately pressed play on all hard-disk recordings from the cameras at once.

The Architect sat for a few minutes at each address, watching intently and then moving off to the next recording. That was until he came to Bruce's recording. You see, there was nothing to see. I explained to The Architect that Bruce only ever went to his famous low-slung house in the desert on weekends. So he asked me to show him the last four weekends' footage. I did so. And the action on screen was the same. Nonexistent. I explained that I had not seen Bruce for a month. I had not heard from him. He had not come into the office to complain. And with that The Architect called Bruce's mobile number. It was turned off. He called

Bruce's work. They reported that they had not seen or heard from him during the previous four weeks. And with that The Architect asked me to pick him up at 8:00 a.m. promptly and drive him to Bruce's desert home.

I did as I was asked. I collected The Architect at exactly 8:00 a.m. on Saturday morning. I had his coffee just the way he liked it and a warm bagel with cream cheese. We drove the four hours without speaking. I inserted my remote controlled iTune earphones and discovered that doing the mundane, listening to music, was in fact not mundane. And in no time at all we were there. Outside Bruce's stunning desert home.

Both The Architect and I walked around the stunning home admiring it in the midday sun. There were no shadows to distract. Just the form against the desert terrain. We sniffed for it. But there was no sign of Bruce except for his locked car, right outside the front door; parked perfectly in the designated space for parking I might add. The Architect pulled a master key from his pocket and we entered. We opened the house to the elements. The windows to thirty-eight degrees. The doors. We set up camp and searched the area in the afternoon light. We could see tracks of wild animals. But that's all we spotted.

Darkness came early to the desert. The temperature dropped, and the sound of everything was amplified. The running of the wind through a branch sounded like a plane taking off. The stars threatened to illuminate and let us see in the dark. And that was when The Architect spotted the fox. He was back on the same old hill. Standing with his head high into the sky. Sniffing the air. Sniffing in the colors of the night.

The Architect walked from Bruce's house, so I followed him. He walked to the ridge. A higher vantage point to see the fox. And that's when he spotted something human crouching on all fours, head faced toward the stars. Baying to the incoming night.

The Architect yelled out and startled the fox and the human. They both turned. The fox ran off. The human lingered for a short time until the fox stopped dead in its tracks and yelped. Then the human ran off after the fox.

The Architect yelled for me to follow him and track them down. But The Architect soon fell in the incoming dark. Stumbling over a rock. He grazed his knuckles. I picked him up and led him back to the glow of Bruce's stunning desert home where we settled for the night. Settled was not a true description of the night. We talked about Bruce all night. About his good points, which only went for around twenty minutes. Then we talked about his failings, and we talked for hours.

In the morning The Architect found a hunter who lived not two hours from Bruce. He hired him to join us track Bruce down.

We were ready before dusk, WiseLED torches at the ready. We had 3,300 lumens of light available in each torch. So we were locked and loaded. We packed water and a small amount of food in case we got hungry. I handmade the sandwiches myself. I packed hand ties and leg ties just in case I had to restrain Bruce. I was hoping I would get to use them.

The Hunter stood on the ridge and looked at the hill where we had spotted the fox and the human. He told us that foxes always returned to their favorite spot, as the territory of this fox would be well marked. Marked with urine and droppings. So he thought the chase should be short, say in a radius of two or three kilometers. And with that I knew my night was going to be shit . Unless I got to tie Bruce up.

As the first pink and purple puffs of cloud tinged the sky the Hunter had us lying on our stomachs against the dirt.

Flat to the earth. He had his Yukon Ranger digital night vision monocular scanning the hill. Ready for the fox hunt. I saw many things wrong with our foxhunt. You see, normally foxes are hunted by men on horseback. We were on foot. They are supported by a pack of foxhounds. The Hunter was supported by The Architect and myself. Normally the hounds follow the scent of the fox. We were following the calling and yelling of the Hunter.

I was hoping the fox would find his lair so we could concentrate on tracking Bruce.

The night started to fall. The fox and the human shared the air on the hill, smelling in the night. The more they sniffed the faster the colors changed.

The Hunter had us crawl for hundreds of yards on our stomach in different directions. So when the fox detected us and ran off, one of us would be in its way. Not to stop the fox, who would have at least fifteen different entrances to his den. But to intercept Bruce. And with that the Hunter set his torch upon the fox. The fox turned quickly like perspiration dripping down a bottle, slow at first and then rapid as it descended. Slightly dazed by the ferocious glow the fox set off. Bruce was slower to react. But he did run. I was initially surprised by Bruce's speed over the desert.

The fox ran straight at The Architect with Bruce on his tail. The fox ran straight through The Architect's legs. Bruce did no such thing. As The Architect held out his open arms to embrace Bruce, Bruce shoulder-charged The Architect, sending him flying through the air, hitting the ground with a thud of dust. The Hunter burst a fuffer valve seeing the Architect fly through the air. His weak, skinny arms trying to grab the running beast that was Bruce.

When the Hunter stopped laughing, after he collected The Architect, the hunt continued. I had joined the group. And we ran as a team.

The Hunter was wiry and tall. Lean. Strong. The sinew of muscle gripping his body like super-glue to a finger. He ran with a purpose. A single-minded thought to track the fox. The Architect was puffed before a couple of minutes. I moved further away from The Architect and closer to the Hunter, who had eyes for the fox; I for Bruce. The fox darted one way then the other while Bruce ran a straight line. The fox was trying to get the Hunter and me and The Architect off Bruce's scent while Bruce made a beeline for his hide.

I had suddenly become a killer of sorts myself, unbeknownst to me. The dark and the night air stripped away all thought other than Bruce's capture. And the longer I pursued Bruce, the stronger my basic instinct to hunt—not for food, not for sport, but for Bruce.

I shined my WiseLED torch in a sweeping motion, capturing every flicker of movement. And that's when I saw Bruce. He had not listened to the fox and stayed hidden. Bruce was looking out to see if I was close, and I was. But I thought it best to masquerade my sighting. So I assumed the role of blind searcher. I moved close to Bruce but not in a straight direct line. I circled him, seeing his hide, a hole in the earth wall of a siding, deep enough just to house Bruce's body. Dirt floor. Dirt walls. Shelter from the sun. But not from the wind. Not from the rain. There was a makeshift wall of brush and bush that hid Bruce's beating heart from me. So I walked by Bruce's hide. I walked past and came back around behind Bruce. I climbed the embankment and stood atop the siding. I stood and waited, WiseLED Torch switched off.

Bruce was very patient, very patient indeed. He waited for what must have been half an hour before he moved the brush and bush covering away, until he stood, back to me, smelling the air. Luckily I was downwind. And that's when I jumped Bruce. I jumped from the height of the siding, both my hands clasped together to resemble a club. I jumped at Bruce and swung my club, hitting Bruce on the back of the neck and head. We both fell heavily to earth. Bruce moaned. I moaned. Bruce turned to look at me as I swung my club again, smashing him in the face. His nose bled instantly. I sat atop Bruce. My body weight against his. My crotch up on his chest. I managed to tie both of Bruce's hands together with the ties. Then I spun around. Edging myself down his torso. Below his groin. Bruce tried to buck me off like a bull bucking its rider, so I slammed myself backward. My back fell heavily onto Bruce's chest. The back of my head slammed into his face, and suddenly there was quiet. I shimmied down Bruce's legs until I had both his feet tied. Then I sat back and felt a strange urge of homoerotica. It was something I had not felt before, but I hoped I would feel it again sometime. I always thought I was asexual. Bruce?

The Hunter came at my call. He had missed the fox, been outsmarted. And he was pissed. The Architect joined us as the Hunter and I were taking photos of each other, standing with one foot on the captured animal, one hand holding the whisky flask, the other hand sternly set in the side pocket of one's hunting jacket. Yes, it was just like any old fox hunt. Victory goes to the man holding the gun.

The Architect screamed when he saw Bruce. I am not certain if it was his bloody nose and swollen face, one eye blackened and closed, or the fact that his fingers and toenails were black and split, broken and scarred. Or the fact that he stunk like a wild animal, smelled of his own feces, his own urine. Yes, Bruce had most definitely marked this territory as his own.

No, The Architect screamed because Bruce was tied up. I explained if I had not put those ties on him he would have run away. But The Architect insisted that I free him. Which I did, and on cue Bruce made a dash for it. The

Hunter raised his stun gun and fired. Bruce went down after the 200 KV of shock surged through his body, which made The Architect scream even more. I could sense that the Hunter was getting annoyed with The Architect's antics, so I took control. I forced some liquid Valium with some water down The Architect's throat. He put up a small fight until I stuck my fingers down past his tongue, releasing him of his anguish. The Hunter and I took Bruce, and we all made it back to Bruce's stunning low-slung desert home.

I walked around outside by myself to calm down. Looking at this place. And I never stopped being amazed at how great the desert looked now that it had an architectural masterpiece to share the space with.

CHAPTER 26.

The Mental Health Act.

We arrived at the home for the mentally insane after dropping The Architect at home. You see, in normal circumstances it takes three people to agree before someone is detained. Bruce was no such someone. All the Hunter had to do was call his mate and Bruce was a patient—a mental patient. I am not saying that Bruce was mental. No, he just needed a little time to rest and recuperate. Think of it as a little enforced holiday.

I stayed and filled in the paperwork, putting myself down as his NR—nearest relative. You see, even though the Hunter's friend, who is an AMHP—approved mental health professional—signed him in, the doctors like to speak to the NR. As Bruce was alone, I figured it was me or the fox, and I wanted to keep the fox out of this. You see, if someone dreams of a fox there is usually someone devious around

169

them. And the last thing Bruce needed was someone devious near him.

Bruce was to be detained for seventy-two hours for initial assessment followed by a subsequent thirty days for total assessment. Bruce's doctors spat out the words that he was to be held for his own health and safety. So treatment started immediately.

I was kept up to speed, day by day, as his NR. I agreed that the maximum six-month holding pattern was ideal for Bruce, so I took over his enduring power of attorney. You see, being detained in itself does not lose you all rights to manage your financial matters or legal affairs. But I thought it only right to relieve Bruce of such pressure. The first thing I did was to freeze Bruce's financial position. I did not want him running overseas and fleeing the country. I managed his bills, his incoming, his outgoings. And right on the three-month mark I realized that Bruce was broke. He had no income, no investments, no immediate chance of earning a dollar unless he wrote his own version of *One Flew over the Cuckoo's Nest*. Which was not going to happen, as Bruce was not mad enough. Yet.

So I did the only thing I could. I sold his desert masterpiece. The price was not market value, but we needed the money now to live and continue treatment. The new owners promised me that they would look after it. And when he came out of hospital, they would offer the property back to Bruce at the same price. So it was more like a tenant looking after the place than a new owner.

All this time The Architect sat in his basement and turned out amazing design after amazing design. Followed by even more amazing designs.

Exactly six months in, Bruce was set free from mental health. All he kept saying was that he wanted to see his low-slung desert palace. So I agreed—who was I to disappoint him? On the drive out with Bruce I could not bring myself to tell him. So I told him about the new owners just before we pulled up. Less stress on Bruce, I thought.

As we pulled into the designated parking spot clearly marked with yellow painted rocks. Bruce noticed all the windows and doors on his masterpiece were open to the wind, and they were not at thirty-eight degrees. There were flags of some sort flying from every window. Bruce ran from the car, ran to the house and entered. All of his beautiful things were gone. I explained that I had gutted the place and put them in storage, for safekeeping.

All that now sat inside were two bunk beds and a rack to hold the guns. I forget to tell Bruce—the new owners were hunters. Fox hunters. They had been there for almost six months and they had cleared the entire desert area of every fox for miles. And with that Bruce put his hands to his ears—here we go again—and screamed ran around in circles. He left me no choice but to stun-gun him.

The hunters helped me get Bruce back in the car. I tied him to the door and made my way back to the hospital. I suddenly realized that in spite of my good wishes for him, poor Bruce was not better yet. I also made note to punish the hunters, but I imagined Bruce would take care of that for me.

Chapter 27.

Too Many Chiefs.

In the meeting room it was clear that Bruce was exhausted, so he sat down. The other two were jostling to spew out the last of their stories so they could go home, or so I thought. The President had been patient, and now it was his turn. He stood as if this was his

final speech, his final opportunity to tell it exactly as it had happened.

He told us that his business was gone, his backers having backed out, seeking a newer, fresher version of himself. They wanted a president without a past, a president with only a future, and with that one statement The President of The Island suddenly fell silent.

Let me take over while he recovers. I knew that the act of The President of The Island handing in his office keys was hard enough. Handing back his mortgage papers and moving out of the family home was the final straw. He and his family had survived thirty years of commercial struggle, but his wife would not survive this. He had been the carpenter working with wood to make something of value. His value was his bank account. And now it was all gone.

He had been the pin-up guy. The guy the magazines stalked. Now he could not get arrested. He had no home. His wife and kids had moved across town without him. He followed them. I followed him during that time. And when I could not I paid a private investigator to stand in my shoes. Luckily I was there to see the family at their first mealtime since they had fled their family home.

The restaurant was full, and there was a line snaking around the corner, which indicated that the restaurant must be good. The restaurant staff did not know who The President was. He was a newcomer. He was well dressed. His suit was perfectly creased. Yes, it would be fair to say he stood out. He also dined alone. Everyone else was either in pairs or groups.

He was constantly watching another group in the restaurant—a mother and her two children. The two tables seemed to know each other, or so the restaurant staff thought. The mother and the two children sat close together, uncomfortable in the restaurant. They shielded their looks. Shielded any invitation to make small talk. In fact they did not speak at all. Not even to each other. It would be an over exaggerated comment to make, but one of the restaurant staff said they looked like three vampires brought into the light for the first time.

The mother and the two children ate quickly, too quickly. They were pleased to be eating in the restaurant, but they hated every second of it.

The President kept eyeballing them. He kept a protective eye over them.

All was calm in the restaurant until the dessert trolley came along, wheeled out like a French Michelin Star establishment. The mother helped herself to three portions, one each for herself and her two children. Then she went back for a fourth. The restaurant staff and the other diners stopped in their tracks, stopped mid-fork. The restaurant fell into silence. The mother walked with one single serving and delivered it to The President of The Island. He accepted it graciously and almost broke into a smile. The mother turned on her heels as quickly as she arrived. The President was heard to say, "Thank you, dear. Thank you," as the mother, his wife, walked back to The President's two children. In the soup kitchen. Run by the local community for the poor and underprivileged. The regular diners were heard to breathe a sigh of relief as status quo had returned.

I watched one of the restaurant staff approach The President and sat down next to him. He stayed for fifteen minutes or so. I asked him when he returned what The President said. He explained that The President spoke in soft words, in a soft tone, without anger. He spoke that his world had been ruined. And he did wipe his eyes as he spoke. He wiped tears that failed to remain in his eyes. Then he took tissues and blew his nose. It was not a flattering thing watching someone blow his or her nose, fingers everywhere in the nostrils, fingering about, collecting all the gunk they can, making sure not to leave any behind. I thought maybe fingers have eyes.

The restaurant worker explained that The President was the husband and father of the two children. I knew that, of course. He explained that they were newly homeless. The wife was bitter, undeserving of this new life. She had done her job, and all she expected of The President was for him to do his. But he had failed—not initially. On the contrary; he had excelled far beyond even her imagination. Now all she wanted was that her old life not stop. But it had. And she found herself there.

The President explained to the restaurant worker that he had found work on the night shift packing shelves in a K-Mart store. He had no work clothes, so during work he removed his tie, jacket, and business shirt. He stood in his white-as-white singlet, his suit trousers, and brogues, packing shelves. It was not well paid. Not appreciated work. Not fulfilling. But it was the start of his way back.

By now his wife and children had left the restaurant quietly, camouflaged by the line of people still waiting to get into the restaurant to dine. I had forgotten for a moment my profession, so I looked hard at the soup kitchen furniture. I imagined it to be donated from an old church. A majority of it was made up of discarded school furniture. Nothing matched. It was eclectic beyond eclectic. Laminex tables were a favorite. They sat alongside folding tables, camp tables, tin tables. The sizes and shapes were disparate. Cutlery was mixed and matched. Large sat with small, silver with faux silver, steel and plastic side by side, Melchior alongside pewter. Everything was utilitarian. Tablecloths were butcher's paper, white yet reddish, made from Kraft pulp. The Kraft process had its advantages, it was stronger than paper made by the pulping process as acidic sulphite processes degrade the cellulose leading to weaker fibers. So it could be used for multiple diners.

The President stood in the middle of the hot room in front of us all telling his story, constantly pausing to clear his throat. To clear his nose. To stop the flow of salt water running down his cheeks.

And it was all that was needed for Bruce to raise himself from him chair and stand next to The President of The Island and start his story again.

Bruce picked up where he left off, in the hospital. I knew

the day I visited Bruce that he was getting better. Yes, the mental institution was working for Bruce, because he was noticing between therapy sessions and medication that the utilitarian architecture of the institution was worrying him. He understood that it was meant to be functional rather than decorative. Bruce had heard the phrase "forms follows function," that "ornament was crime." And the day I visited he was worried that the white paint was not really white and it was not a consistent white. Newer walls showed whiter white paint being glossier, not flat like the other walls. Bruce remembered The Architect say that painting a room white gives it depth, that different shades of white highlight architectural detail, that white is the perfect backdrop for color contrast, that cloud white is the chameleon of white, taking on the colors of the day. Bruce remembered hearing about white being tinted with ivory, chalk, cream, antique paper, beige, blue, and yellow. That there were more than one hundred whites to choose from. Bruce told me about the cold white LED light above him. About the blue-glowing chip coated with a layer of phosphor that when excited by the blue light glowed yellow, making a cold shade of white. Bruce commented on the hospital paintings. The walls groaned with paintings by former patients and by the famous mentally ill. There seemed to be copies of Picasso's *Weeping Woman* on corridors everywhere. Jackson Pollock was featured, being bipolar himself. Edward Davies, also being bipolar, was there alongside Edvard Munch. The clinical depression of Toulouse Lautrec was there. Monet. Van Gogh. Rothko. Yes, the walls were mad for it. And Bruce knew it.

When Bruce told me this during my NR visit I knew he was well enough to leave this place. And with that I signed him out. I found him a job and a flat above his new job place. I left Bruce alone for a while to recuperate. He deserved the time alone.

In front of the group Bruce stopped speaking when he dropped his folder of papers, his folder of dead bodies. Dead corpses. He scrambled and fell to his knees on the floor, picking them up one by one. Making sure not to crease them. Putting them in perfect order.

Which gave Wild Bill the opportunity to finish off, so to speak. Wild Bill stood three abreast in the center of the room next to the President and the kneeling Bruce. I was the only audience. I enjoyed my celebrity status. I encouraged Wild Bill to continue.

Wild Bill explained that his time had been completely overtaken by the new gallery opening. Business was business. Money was to be made. So Wild Bill concentrated day and night on creating an art event that every respected buyer would swarm to. Wild Bill created the website, infiltrated art organizations. Spoke to newspaper art critics and art publications. He paid to be interviewed on television. He paid for advertising. He flushed out the new media. He hired graffiti artists to paint abstract references to the gallery on walls across town. He had a local rock band write a song, shoot a clip, and post it on YouTube. He printed programs on the finest paper. Bought the best wine. Hired the best caterer. Tasted canapés by the dozen to decide on the right combination. Wild Bill worked tirelessly to organize the media. He knew that the ensuing publicity was essential in making the gallery opening a success. The art critic of the *New York Times* was coming. The *Times Magazine* art critic. *The New York Observer.* Wild Bill knew to make himself available.

Available. Wild Bill knew that everyone who came along was worth talking to. Plus Wild Bill knew his Artist intimately. He knew what he liked to eat, that he could cook, that his upbringing was underprivileged, that he was challenged. But tonight was his coming out.

Wild Bill knew that he had the suavity to convince someone to acquire—buy is such a hard word—something that had no apparent function in life. To acquire *art*.

Wild Bill realized quickly what his job was. His new job was a service to the Artist, a service to his soon-to-be clients. Yes, the Artist was his partner, now so much more than just a houseguest. Wild Bill would introduce the Artist to every buyer, so he knew who had acquired his work.

Wild Bill knew he had an obligation to pay the artist before himself, which prompted Wild Bill to say loudly, "You never pay yourself before you pay your Artist."

But beyond all of this Wild Bill knew the Artist was "the next big thing." The *New York Times* said it five years earlier. It's just that now, now, was his time.

The night had come, the night of nights for Wild Bill and the Artist. Trophy was the trophy she always was, on the end of an arm from the big end of town. Leaving home, Trophy walked down the stairs in her house in slow motion. She was ravishing. Both Wild Bill and the Artist stood speechless. Only one of them felt the twang of sexual energy run through his groin. But he controlled it, like he had done many times before. Trophy wore a shirtdress by Gucci. It was a shirt to the waist, where it gathered for a centimeter and then fell to her knees. The fabric was begonia silk crepe de chine with cherry-colored satin details. It was 100 percent silk. The shirtdress highlighted her face and neck, her legs and feet— the extremes, as I like to call them. Her hands were partly covered by the extra-length fabric than touched her palms and fingers. The dress flowed around her. It flowed over her pert breasts, showing their form, over her bottom, perfect as it was, high enough to know there was room to drop.

As she walked down the stairs to an uncommon silence, the fabric swished around her. Yes, it swished. Both Wild Bill and the Artist told me so. Even on the video I could see the swish. Hear the swish. Tonight the swish was Trophy. And Trophy was the swish.

Wild Bill stumbled for a second before the group. Swallowed the additional saliva that had accumulated in his throat. He paused. And that's all it took.

The President jumped into his grave like one of the three tenors waiting for the exact moment to come in. And he did. The President's throat was cleared. I wasn't sure if there was a throat bug in the room. But I felt fine. I swallowed a few times to make certain. There was no burn, no pain. So the three tenors standing before me must all be racing to bring this thing to an end.

The President explained how his wife and kids planned their days and weeks so they could avoid him. He had become the rat that soiled their office. So now he was on his own, especially during the hours when the kids were at school and his wife was at work. That's the time The President broke into their small council apartment and sat alongside the photos of his family. It's the time he smelled his wife's clothes packed neatly in the suitcases. The time he checked his kids' school books. The time he made sure they were keeping their grades. He wanted so much to correct their essays and papers and leave them notes to point out their mistakes. But he knew he must not. He knew he must not show his hand with them, or they would change the locks and move away without telling him. So The President sat. Every day. In the public housing apartment where they lived. Looking around, staring at the walls. The President noticed clearly the thing that differed between the rich and the poor. It was not the materials used to build and finish the apartment; it was the workmanship. He also knew that the very same workers who worked on these apartments worked on The Island. On the homes of the rich. There the workers worked by the hour, being painstakingly amazing with their finishes, while here, in the apartment blocks, they were paid by the job. So they rushed. Glued things when they should have been nailed or doweled. Stapled things when they should have been nailed. The laminate was badly installed. The cornices were ill fitted. The power points were crooked. The light fittings were not flush. The toilet was not square on the floor. The taps leaked. The shower screens stuck. The timber floating floors actually floated and had waves.

Everything about the poor was shoddy.

The President left an hour before his family was due home. He did this every day for weeks. He did this until yesterday. Yes, yesterday. Yesterday was different. The President walked to the public housing apartment as he always did. He picked the cheap lock and went inside. But there was nothing there. The housing apartment was empty. The President ran to his wife's work. They said that she had quit. She has resigned four weeks earlier, and yesterday was her last day. They had no idea where she had gone. They were sorry. The President ran to his children's school. Of course all the staff knew of him from his past life when he was the real President of The Island. They refreshed him with water, a tissue. They calmed him before telling him that his children had not come to school that day, that the Headmaster had received a note from the President's wife. It explained the trauma was too much for the children to bear. So she was taking them away until the situation changed.

The other tenors stood on stage and looked at the floor instead of the audience. They stood as if they had forgotten their words. And no one jumped in to finish their own story. The President stood for a long time and swallowed hard. He took off his spectacles and folded them carefully, placing them in his jacket pocket. Then he put his right hand deep into his pants pocket, locating what he was looking for. The President of The Island found a pocket gun. I did not know if it was a Beretta, an Airweight snubnose, a 32, or a Derringer. The President took it and held it against his right temple. The President knew that the pocket gun had little accuracy so he pushed it hard into his skin. None of us moved to stop him. It might sound strange. But none of us thought we had the right. The President was a smart man. But he knew he had become the rat in the night that shits and pisses and roots on everything fine.

The President closed his eyes as he pulled the trigger.

The noise of the firing made us all jump. But it was the aftermath that touched us all. All of us were splattered. Splattered by small drops of red goo. I did not see how it was possible. The two tenors both stood to his left, so I guessed that was possible. But I sat out in front. It must have been the result of him being swung around after the bullet had entered the bone around his temple as it smashed its way through the temporal bone and the sphenoid bone. I'm not certain if it went through his temporal lobe, but it must have been when The President swung around that I got splattered. Either way I knew I had some cleaning up to do before we could continue.

I wet some cloths and handed them to Bruce and Wild Bill so they could clean themselves. I knew that bloodstains are permanent once they set. I knew that hot water was a no-no. I rinsed the cloths in cold water and added liquid soap. Then all that was needed was a little elbow grease.

The ambulance came and took The President away. I cleaned the floor area and asked who would like to continue. Bruce jumped in. As I knew he would.

Bruce explained that he loved his new job. He was the official taxidermist's assistant. An assistant just like me. Bruce explained that taxidermy originally came from the Greek word meaning skin. I quickly realized that if anyone was going to get under people's skin it was Bruce. Bruce explained that taxidermy could be achieved on any vertebrate—mammals, birds, fish, reptiles. He explained that taxidermists work for museums. Hunters. Fishermen and hobbyists. And to practice taxidermy one must be very familiar with anatomy.

I smiled on the inside as Bruce spoke. He spoke with the same vitality as he had the day I first met him. He fumbled and moved on the spot. He tugged at the underpants that tried to creep up his ass crack. He tried to speak far too quickly for his mouth to accommodate. But I understood the majority of his rant. Bruce explained that taxidermists could also supply magnificent life-like replica animals. Then he explained there was even mummification of humans. Well, not really, Bruce explained; it was actually embalming of humans, the process of chemically treating the dead to reduce the presence and growth of microorganisms to inhibit organic decomposition.

Bruce explained his new job in great detail. He described it with love. And passion. And precision. Bruce explained that anybody to be embalmed is first laid flat, facing upward. The arms are put into position and Bruce had a few favored positions. The eyes are left open, or closed. Bruce then drooled as he spoke about the insertion of the arterial solution directly into the main artery and corresponding vein. How the fluid flowed into the dead body via the cannula inserted into the artery under pressure. The fluid circulated, pushing out all the blood from the veins. Bruce collected the blood. It was meant for disposal. But Bruce kept it. Then Bruce sutured the incision holes in the neck and groin.

Next was the cavity embalming. Bruce was taught to use a "trocar," a large hollow tube with a sharp end. Bruce inserted it into the dead person's abdomen. He found the organs, punctured them, and sucked them out via the hollow tube. Bruce sucked out the insides: the lower esophagus, the stomach, the duodenum, the jejunum, the Ileum, the cecum, the appendix, the four colons—ascending, transverse, descending, and sigmoid. The rectum, the liver, the kidneys, the pancreas, and the spleen. Bruce had always been good at vacuuming, he said, and this job was no exception. He went into detail about holding the embalming fluid above his head to let gravity to its job. Then he explained how he inserted a small "trocar button" into the puncture hole to close it up and prevent leakage. Next Bruce washed the naked body. Shampooed the hair. Or not. Cleaned the fingernails. Or not. Moisturized the face. Or not.

Bruce's new boss had loaned him the five thousand dollars to complete the course so he could be his assistant. He liked Bruce so much he let him work alone.

Wild Bill was tired of standing, so he sat down while Bruce was speaking. His legs now hurt all the time. And when Bruce stopped speaking to find a photograph of a dead body to show us all, Wild Bill jumped up.

Wild Bill explained that during the chauffeured drive to the gallery opening it was quiet, too quiet. There was nervous energy, but it was internalized. Like everyone was holding in a fart and if they spoke or moved it would come out. I reviewed the footage from the in car camera. It was reinforced. They all seemed to be holding in a fart. But everyone had a very different look on their faces. Trophy looked composed. Wild Bill and the Artist looked pained.

You see, men and women are very different. The physical differences are obvious. Trophy was stunning. Her skin was blemish free, smooth. Her lips were full and red. Her eyes small and clear. In contrast to women, men are made for survival. Their upper body is strong. Muscular. Their skin is thicker. They bruise less easily. Their joints are made for throwing things. Their skulls are thicker. They are more reckless. Women on the other hand have four times as many neurons connecting the right side to the left side of their brain. Women can focus on multiple problems. But not tonight. Trophy was focused on one.

Wild Bill and the Artist were male to the core. Males approach problems with the same goal as females, but their approach is anything but similar. Women concern themselves with how problems are solved, men with solving them. This solving of problems can weaken or strengthen a relationship. But for tonight they were a threesome.

The car door opened to a distinct lack of cameras and flashes, to a distinct lack of red carpet and paparazzi. The car door opened to the three of them laying everything on the line. Once inside Wild Bill was his old self. He schmoozed and shook hands, welcomed people, and started his three hundred introductions. "Good evening. So pleased you could make it. This is the star himself. The Artist. Please, any questions—I am your man. And feel free to ask the Artist anything. Anything."

Trophy followed Wild Bill like a flowing scarf pulled tight around his neck, a scarf that flowed three feet behind his shoulders. Trophy was unaware of the envious looks she received from both men and women. Men thought how lucky Wild Bill was. Women thought how her beauty would soon leave her, except for a few small injections and skin pulling and eye tightening. Ah, the thrill of having many beautiful women in one roof was intoxicating. As Picasso said, "Women are either to sleep with or paint."

The night went well, really well. Every painting had a red dot on it. Every painting was sold for the asking price—no discount tonight. The buyers were ready to make out the checks when Trophy stood close by Wild Bill and spoke for the first time that evening.

"Wild Bill, you said you would always pay the Artist before yourself, so why don't you let the Artist hold the checks tonight? Even if it is just for tonight."

Wild Bill was taken aback. He looked at the beaming faces in front of him and went one further. "Why don't you make the checks out to the Artist himself? And he can pay me."

Everyone laughed, cheered, clinked champagne glasses. And with that it was done. The Artist was handed his due, checks totaling over eight hundred thousand dollars. It was more than he had held in his hands in his life. It was bigger than Trophy's tits. Bigger than Bev's ass. But it did the opposite. It did not weight him down. He felt as light as a feather holding the money. There was backslapping in the room and assurances that Wild Bill would let the same buyers buy at the next showing. Everyone went home with a smile on their face.

The next morning Wild Bill woke. Trophy was not next to him. He did not remember her getting up, but the hard liquor he toasted the Artist with late last night might have something to do with that. Wild Bill stretched his nostrils as far as his nose muscles would let him, but he smelled no cooked breakfast. Maybe the Artist also had a headache as big as Bev's ass.

Wild Bill moved gingerly down the stairs. All was quiet. He did not have the energy or the inclination or the vocal strength to call out and search for Trophy. She would come to his side as she always did. She might stray for an hour, but she would always be back. Wild Bill tiptoed down to the Artist's dungeon, opening the door in the hope that Trophy was not asleep or awake beside the Artist. But she was not. And he was not. The Artist was also up and about. Maybe Trophy and the Artist were in the sauna? No. In the pool house? No. In the garden? No. Sunbaking next to each other around the pool? No. Maybe they had gone out to buy a celebratory breakfast and bring it home for Wild Bill? And with that thought Wild Bill sat in the sun, sunglasses on, with a glass of the fresh concoction the artist always left in the fridge for him.

CHAPTER 28.

Time Frames.

It was now Wild Bill who showed he was also worse for wear. He looked as tired as Bruce did. So while they both rest and take a well-earned break, let me explain one more thing. The Architect took approximately one year to pull the puppeteer strings from the day he turned the cameras on and forced himself into his clients' lives.

But now, in this room, there were just the three of us. No more President of The Island, as he was dead. No Architect, as he wasn't invited. Just Wild Bill, Bruce and myself.

So more than a few things had changed in that year. Like Wild Bill's overweight body. I would have called it obese, but his BMI was borderline. It was twenty-six. And, yes, you guessed it, two and six equals eight.

Wild Bill had not seen Trophy or the Artist ever again. Not the first day they were missing, not the next week. Or the next month. Trophy and the Artist had disappeared. The fabulous lunches and dinners prepared by the Artist had disappeared with them. Wild Bill started to tell it in his own words to the group. But I am more impartial, so let me tell you.

Wild Bill was not worried about Trophy until it became dark that first evening. She had disappeared. She was not at the gym. Not at the hairdresser. Not at the nail salon. Not at the Botox clinic. Not having liposuction. So where was she? The first night after 8:00 Wild Bill went to the police station to report her missing. He knew the law and knew that he did not have to wait twenty-four hours to report her missing. But he did forget some of the simple rules. The reporting officer asked him for a recent photo. Wild Bill fumbled through his wallet and found nothing. He searched his phone but found only revealing, naked shots of Trophy taken when she wasn't aware. He had photos of the Artist's paintings featuring Trophy. But the names might suggest the wrong thing. So he described her. Physically. Her hair color as it was then and her natural color. He explained her height by showing the officer that her head came up to his chin. The officer got a ruler and measured to the bottom of Wild Bill's chin. The officer asked if Wild Bill had shoes on when Trophy measured to his chin. Wild Bill answered no. He neglected to tell the officer that it was when they were intimate, in the eagle's nest, that he noticed that Trophy came up to his chin. It was when she sucked on his nipples like a little pig feeding off its fat mother. Yes, he neglected to tell him that. But I saw it all. Wild Bill said he would drop in a photo later that evening.

He explained that the last time he saw Trophy was when he went to bed. He explained that the house had not been broken into, that the area was triple-A secure. The suburb had its own police force. It was they who had sent Wild Bill to the station. Wild Bill explained that he did not know whom she might be with. Then it occurred to him that the Artist was also missing. And so was the cash from last night. Wild Bill explained that he had phoned all the places she would normally visit and that she had been missing from those places as well. Wild Bill went home. Empty-handed.

Wild Bill went straight to the Artist's dungeon. His personal things were gone. But he had left his animals in the freezer, the animals that had touched Trophy's body. Wild Bill licked the prairie fox's tongue, which had touched Trophy's crotch. He licked where Trophy sat on the back of the dog that was as big as a horse. He licked the cougar's tongue, which had touched Trophy's nipple. And all the pleasure he got from it was the taste of frozen animal fur in his mouth. The taste was stronger than anything he could remember, and it was definitely not of Trophy. Wild Bill sat on the freezer room floor with the bad taste in his mouth and cried like a little girl.

You see, Wild Bill was now more of a girl than his old self. And the Artist had a lot to do about that. He was hired to do a job, and he did it. The concoction the Artist made for Wild Bill every day contributed to Wild Bill generating a massive dose of estrogen. Yes, males have estrogen in small, balanced amounts, and estrogen is actually a by-product of the testosterone-conversion process. Those "balanced levels" of estrogen in men are essential to encourage healthy libido. Protect the heart. Strengthen bones. While high levels of estrogen caused reduced testosterone. Fatigue. Loss of muscle tone. Increased body fat. Loss of libido. Loss of and sexual function. And result in an enlarged prostate, let alone shutting down the normal testicular production of testosterone.

The excessive estrogen inside Wild Bill saturated his testosterone receptors, making his gonads or balls, inactive.

They literally shut down. Yes, Wild Bill was also on his way to diabetes, thanks to the Artist.

But what seemed to disturb him most was that Wild Bill had no one to cook for him and no one to eat with. So he ate in his car. He ate out. He ate in the dark. He ate in car parks. He ate in movie theaters. He ate junk food. He ate every minute he felt depressed, which was all the time. Wild Bill ate while he walked around his monstrous home alone. He ate a burger or a chicken nugget for each room in the house. Thirty-eight rooms made Wild Bill satisfied until his next craving. Then Wild Bill washed it all down with a six-pack of energy beer. Which is what he had done every day since Trophy went missing.

That was until Wild Bill waddled to the front fence and collected his mail from his gold-plated mailbox with the eight-digit laser lock. There it was—overseas mail; a postcard inside an envelope from France. Whom did Wild Bill know in France? No one. So he ripped the envelope open. It was from Paris, from Montmartre. It was not signed. Rather it was painted. The painting on the front of the postcard was of Montmartre. The backside of the postcard looked blank, but it was also painted in glow-in-the-dark acrylic paint. Wild Bill did not know that until 1:08 a.m. the following morning as he went downstairs to drain the last of the concoction the Artist had made for him. He drank the very last drop, wiping his finger around the glass to inhale the last of the wonderful-tasting mix, and that's when he saw the ink glow in the dark. In fact it was not painted; it was handwritten. The words were quite hard to make out. So Wild Bill rushed back with a black light. He read them out aloud to himself: "Bill. I use that as your name as you are no longer wild. No. You are now more of a woman than a man. Don't believe me? Then have your estrogen checked. It will reveal your balls no longer make testosterone. You already know your dick no longer works.

And by now you must have just about finished the last of the concoction. I bet you look fat in your naked skin. It is just what you deserve. Signed The Artist and T."

"The Artist and T. The Artist and T. *The Artist and T!*"

Wild Bill was now yelling. Repeating it over and over again. And again. And again. Then he looked at the postcard again. There was a PS. It read: "Wild (with a straight line through the word wild) Bill, I like your feminine side."

And with that Wild Bill fell to his fat knees on his thousand-dollar-a-meter tiles and wept. He did not cry. That is for a dignified person. He wept, a kind of a woman's weep.

The next morning Wild Bill rushed to the police station with the postcard, but alas the glow in the dark ink only had a short life and the life had run out of it. The police officer looked at him and ascertained that he was a rich man, and that's when he asked Wild Bill the age of Trophy. Wild Bill had to think a little. She was twenty-two years younger than he was. So if Wild Bill was fifty-four, Trophy was thirty-two. Then he asked how old the Artist was. Wild Bill replied in a second: Thirty-five. Remember that Wild Bill knew everything about his artist. Well, almost everything. And with that the officer handed Wild Bill back his postcard and went about his business.

CHAPTER 29.

The Smell of Formaldehyde in the Morning.

Wild Bill could not continue. So he waddled his fat body over to the chair that could no longer eat him, leaving Bruce alone center stage.

Bruce continued to tell us about his new life. He told us with glee how he woke to his new best smell. It wasn't coffee or the smell of a woman. His new smell of choice was formaldehyde. Bruce knew of its use in earlier years as a preserving agent. But now it was deemed to have carcinogenic properties. So Bruce just sniffed it upon waking. It did his sinuses a world of good. It was good for warts. And it killed most bacteria.

Bruce used it mainly for his rapidly growing collection of smaller animals, for embalming, although he found nothing wrong using it on bigger specimens.

Bruce worked all day in the taxidermy studio downstairs. As his mentor was now in his sixties, Bruce had free run most of the time. Nighttime was used for his personal projects. He was an artist of sorts. He would never admit it himself, but I saw it in him.

The first time I broke into Bruce's flat above the taxidermy store I marveled at his craftsmanship, at his eye for detail. In the glass cases that lined Bruce's apartment there were taxidermy mice, rats, cats, small dogs. And in the gold case with the spotlight shining on it was his star of the show: Mr. Fox. His coat was reddish with streaks of white. Mr. Fox in fact looked like he had highlights in his fur. I imagined Bruce setting foils like a hairdresser. In fact, I was right. Bruce had researched the rules of adding highlights to hair—in this case, fur. Bruce parted the dry hair of Mr. Fox with one hand and with his tail comb chose a piece of fur; with the other hand Bruce grabbed the foil and slid the comb up under the section of fur, making certain it was taut. Bruce then applied the color, in this case white, to the fur; then he folded the foil in thirds. Bruce repeated this down the chest of Mr. Fox. Then he repeated it on the center of his long snout. For the snout there was little fur to grab, so Bruce painted the white directly to the fur.

Mr. Fox stood in the spotlight on all fours, his head twisted high, smelling in the colors of the night. Bruce had set up a small fan disguised inside a rock on the fake desert floor Mr. Fox stood proudly on. The fan blew Mr. Fox's fur just like the evening breeze did when Bruce stood near him on the hill. Bruce had painted a purple night sky inside the glass box. Stars dotted the purple like hypnotic lanterns. Bruce lamented to himself that those were the best days of his life.

I also noticed three large glass cases that stood empty. They were approximately eight feet high and the width of a chair. I was intrigued. I wanted to know Bruce's every whereabouts in case I was a target for one of the big glass boxes, so I hid a GPS locating device on Bruce's car. For under two hundred dollars I had a tracker that downloaded a complete movement history, it was so small that I could have set it on his windscreen. But I didn't. Then all I had to do was connect it to my computer and Bruce's every move was mine.

It didn't take long before the GPS started moving on my computer. But instead of waiting to see where Bruce was headed, I followed. I wanted to see what was going on with my own eyes.

Bruce drove straight for the desert and his low-slung home. There was a storm predicted, so I was glad I had my rainwear in the car. When he arrived it was heading toward dusk. Bruce set up near Mr. Fox's den, not that he used it anymore. With him Bruce brought two things. The first was a FoxPro. The FoxPro was a digital remote-controlled game call featuring twenty-four high-quality fox sounds.

The second thing Bruce brought with him was man-made lightning. To be precise it was an LIPC, or a laser-induced plasma channel. Some people called it an electrical air-gap spark machine, as it used precursor laser pulses to burn a conductive tunnel through the air, down which an electrical charge jumps. Which meant Bruce could aim his lightning gun, or man-made lightning, and fire it to kill a human right there, in the desert.

Bruce had methodically researched how his embalming patients had died, which taught him how to kill. Bruce discovered that all he needed to do was interrupt the human heart rhythm for three seconds; then the heart went arrhythmic, which caused everything else in the body to shut down.

The weather in the desert had turned just as Bruce and the

weatherman had predicted. It was almost sunset when Bruce sent out his first fox call from the FoxPro. The megaphone projecting the sound pointed straight at Bruce's low-slung masterpiece. It stopped the two hunters in their tracks. They had cleared the area of every fox, but now there seemed to be an intruder. Smiles broke over their faces as they dressed for the incoming weather, loaded their guns, and called back to Bruce's machine with their open-reed calls. Yes, the hunters held a hand caller. An open-reed caller is handheld, and by blowing through the reed a hunter can make many sounds, from puppy yelps to bird calls. But the sound they made was to lure a fox. What they didn't know was they themselves were being lured.

Bruce sat a short distance away from the FoxPro, in full camouflage. He looked like a cross between a small mound of dirt and a desert shrub. He wore night goggles as he watched the two critters approach from the direction of his desert home.

The two animals that approached Bruce were mammalia. Their order was primate, like the apes. Their family was Hominidae, meaning without tail. Their subfamily was Homininae. Their tribe was Hominini. Their genus was Homo. Scientifically speaking they were Homo Sapiens. But Bruce knew them as pure animals, killers, carnivores.

As the hunters approached and got closer Bruce sent out another call, and they dropped to the ground, sneaking on their torsos through the dirt, blowing their open-reed and giving their position away. Yes, Bruce could see them clearly.

The hunters crept up on the FoxPro. They crept up on it until they could almost see it. They could smell that there was something wrong. In the back of their minds they knew they had been called by a machine, so they stood. One of the hunters spotted the FoxPro, picked it up, and threw it to the ground. Smashing it. And that's when Bruce stood up, screaming and yelling like a banshee. The Hunters jumped from fright, looking at the clump of earth and brush that had a voice. Bruce loved the scared look on their faces, but that was nothing compared to their faces when he opened fire on them with his trusty man-made lightning gun directed by the laser pulses. It was one almighty shot that hit each of them. One almighty shot of high-voltage electric current.

The hunters seemed to be instantly glued to the desert earth they stood on, twitching. Their hair smoked. Their skin glistened. Their faces convulsed. They bit their tongues. Their eyes rolled. They seemed to dance like puppets on a string as Bruce stood there, amused, watching them jiggle. Then, just like that, they fell onto the ground, dead as doornails.

The approaching storm and desert lightning was the perfect cover. Killed by lightning, the autopsy report would state; that's if they ever found the bodies or if anyone reported them missing. Not that these hunters had next of kin; Bruce was sure of it. Bruce was certain the hunters probably fucked the dead foxes or each other. So there was no one to come looking for them.

I almost applauded from my hide after watching Bruce's performance of excellence, and Bruce must have sensed it. He turned and fired the lightning gun in my direction. The bolt hit the ground near me. I almost pissed myself with both pleasure and the dire need to urinate. So I skulked away to a safer vantage point when I could.

I watched Bruce as he walked to his magnificent home, taking the hunter's truck keys. Driving it to pick up their bodies. Then Bruce drove back to his desert house. He closed all the windows and all the doors. He swept the floors and wiped everything over with a damp cloth and locked up his house. Safe. In the desert. I was guessing it was now his once more.

Back at Bruce's apartment I watched him and found him to be a real artist. Yes, an artist. Not like The Architect. Not like the Artist. But an artist of moral preservation.

Firstly Bruce laid the hunters face down on their stomachs. He took their clothes off. Then with almost surgical precision Bruce inserted a thin metal rod up through their anus and threaded it all the way up to the base of their neck. He joined and bound their feet so the metal pole was invisible when viewed from the front. Bruce flipped them over and spritzed their faces with a solution. He explained everything to himself, talking as he went, speaking through each step. Bruce mumbled that their eyes and nose and mouth were now disinfected. Bruce looked at the unshaven faces and trimmed the beards to a close shave as he knew their beards would continue to grow even though they were dead. Bruce kept both their eyes open as well as their mouths. Then Bruce lined their mouths with a mixture of cotton wool, barbed wire, and wadding. He put his hand inside the mouth, like a dentist, while holding the outside cheek with his other hand, asserting pressure. He rammed the clump of wadding until it was in place, stuck fast to the inside skin. The result was a grimace on the face, an expression of fear. Bruce worked with the feature fixer to make their faces rather plump, like Botox. Then via a hole he made in the neck, Bruce located the carotid artery, tying it off with string. He used the jugular vein to pump in the embalming fluid. And with that he worked throughout the night. Massaging the limbs and face of the hunters to make certain the blood flowed out and the embalming fluid flowed in.

I could not keep pace with Bruce. I watched the camera emitting pictures back to my computer most of the night. However, I fell asleep, and when I woke Bruce had finished. Two of the empty glass cabinets in his apartment were no longer empty; they housed their captured prey. Bruce wanted them as prized possessions in his collection. He wanted them as the hunted, not the hunters. So Bruce had set about attaching the small rodents and relatives of Mr. Fox to their faces, to their groins, as if the animals were frozen mid-attack on the defenseless hunters. Yes, frozen. And that's just what they were as Bruce turned on the refrigeration units to keep them cool. And with that Bruce had obviously stopped for breath and went to bed without a shower. The smell of formaldehyde ringing strong in his nostrils.

I sighed with temporary relief. But there was still one glass case empty.

CHAPTER 30.

Neglected.

I had planned to divert the office phones to my cell phone as I walked out at the end of the very long night spent watching Bruce and saw the one thing I had neglected.

The Architect's light was on in the basement. I knew this because I turned and saw his image in the control room window. The reflection from the camera showed The Architect drawing and designing. It showed The Architect among hundreds of sheets of hummingbird sketches. I had totally neglected him. How long exactly he had been drawing I could not remember. When had he last eaten? When had he last showered? And with that I rushed in. The air rushing into the room with me startled The Architect. It did not stop the constant playing of Beethoven. I cocked my ear and remembered it was the eighth symphony. But it did stop The Architect. His pencil just froze in his hand. Exhausted. I did not ask any questions. I picked him up as if I had super-human strength and carried him to my car, his head resting on mine, his mouth so dry he could barely drip spittle. I drove him to his home, carried him inside, ran a bath, and washed his fully clothed body, as I could not bring myself to see The Architect's penis just in case the black jelly was modeled on it. Then I sat him on his closed toilet while I blow-dried him, clothes and all. It took me almost an hour to dry him all over. I shaved him. Did his hair. Fed him soup, and put him to bed.

I raced back to the office to forage through the drawings. Sleep would not deprive me of seeing his magic.

My heart almost stopped as I held the brilliance in my hands. The brilliance leaped from the pages. Monumental pillars of stone. The power and the glory of church-like domes. The soaring of bricks and mortar. Buildings that curved away from themselves, before staring back at themselves. Airport hangar-like spaces that bent the mind and space. Brutish raw concrete. Kinetic constructions that reached high into the sky and reeked of permanence. Buildings that incorporated science, art, and design. Amusingly and disturbingly warped shapes. Houses that borrowed from the *Star Wars* fleet of spaceships. A house that mirrored the dragonfly. A city that mirrored *The Jetsons*. Designs based on origami (if The Architect could fold it, then he could build it). Homes just twelve-feet wide and sixty-feet high. Straight lines drawn in every direction toward the sun, sunning themselves. Houses that resembled an insect nest. Flowers. Spider webs. A set of binoculars with viewing ports as eyes.

I fell to my knees. And breathed. I needed to remind myself to breathe. In. Out. Out longer. In deeper. I catalogued everything. Put them in order. Repositioned his hummingbird pencils. Restacked his white-as-white paper. Cleaned around his workspace until everything was as it should be.

I went back to The Architect's home eight hours later and woke him. Fed him. Then set him back to sleep. I decided to stay and watch him. To try to suck all and any spare creativity he had to give. I watched him dribble while he slept. I mopped it up and put it in a vial. I marked it and dated it. I went through his bathroom and took the hair fibers that sat in his hairbrush, dating them. I remember the first time I came to his house when I looked in his trash and found a discarded toothbrush. I took it. I took note of the empty cans and packages of food in the trash. I decided to change my diet and eat just like him in order to make myself more like him. I fingered the clothes in his wardrobe, taking note of brands. Underpants. Singlets. Socks. But today I found The Architect's diary. I read it from front to back. In between helping him to the toilet. Feeding him. And putting him back to bed.

I reread about his life growing up. His parents. The penises. Mia. His money from the adult shops. I read about me, how he had huge expectations of me. I beamed a smile broad enough to encompass his dressing table. The Architect wrote about his clients. He named them all. He named his favorites. Bruce. Wild Bill. He wrote about them inhabiting his homes, his designs. He asked on the page if they were okay. So I made a point to tell him they were fine, all of them, living happy content lives in his masterpieces. And when I whispered all this information to him while he slept he seemed to sigh with relief and fell back into an even deeper sleep.

He slept with a contentment I had not seen. A contentment that seemed to radiate from his face. His body. A contentment that made him smile even as he slept.

I reread more of the diary and read about The Architect's celibacy. I knew it. He had no time for sex. For partners. And in that I was just like him.

I tucked him in once more and left him. Smiling.

The next thing I did was shop. I shopped like The Architect. I shopped at his shops. I bought the very same brands, the very same style of clothes, the same sizes, the same colors. My wardrobe was a mirror image of The Architect's. For all anyone knew, I was him.

CHAPTER 31.

Business as Usual.

The meeting room was restless for the last time. It was two thirty in the morning. Wild Bill had little to add to his story but to say that he had sold his stunning designer home and he intended to move to a retirement home for rich people, in the sun. Yes, besides being alone, divorced, and fat, Wild Bill was still rich.

Bruce explained that he had taken over the taxidermy business from his mentor who retired. Plus he had taken back ownership, albeit unofficially, of his stunning desert home, and for the first time looked confident. His underpants no longer rode up his ass crack, as I found out later, toward the end of the session, he went to the bathroom and ripped them off, going commando.

And with the end in sight I stood in the tiny hot room where we had revealed everything about The Architect and wrote in huge letters in marker on the wall the one phrase that would echo forever in Bruce's and Wild Bill's life. I wrote:

BE YOURSELF. IF YOU ARE FAT BE FAT. IT YOU ARE MENTAL BE MENTAL.

I felt their stares on my back, the stares that looked through me. The stares that looked beyond the clothes I wore. They stared at me as they tried to work out if I was him. If I was The Architect. But it was my roman nose that let them know that for all of the things I tried to be I was not him.

And with that the three tenors hugged each other. It was kind of awkward hugging another man, because men seem to push their groins forward when they hug, unlike women who push their butts away from the cuddler, to protect themselves I imagine.

Oh, I almost forgot to tell you. Trophy and the Artist were living together in Paris, and they too were celibate like The Architect and me. Trophy thought that if they could love each other without sex, then they were in love for real.

So the meeting had come to an end. I felt a relief of sorts. I had been involved in their lives for so long. I had pulled the strings, but none of them knew it. But now I had to pay attention to being the new me. I had a new wardrobe to wear. My new hairstyle to coif. And I finally knew who I was.

The next day I was in the office early as usual. The Architect was holed up in his basement, secure, as I had retrieved him just yesterday to return to work. I delivered his morning coffee, waiting for him to drink and agree on its temperature. The Architect took a second glance at me as he said good morning. He smiled at me. And I felt good.

I went to the control room and watched The Architect sip his coffee again. Then I watched him start to draw like the hummingbird. I automatically locked the door leading to his basement for his own good, so no one could interrupt him. And I thought what a world apart today was from yesterday.

The sun rose this morning with no knowledge of what had happened the day before. No recognition of those who were hurt or who left us. It rose just like it did every other day. It shone on the lucky ones as they walked to work, as they drove to work, as they sat and laughed during their work break, as they drank their lattes. While it burned the unlucky.

I had arrived in the office dressed exactly like The Architect. And when he was ensconced in his designing I put on the shiny bits, the flashy bits, the bits that I never thought I could ever wear. I knew where he hid them, and I thought that today was the day I would encompass my phrase of independence from last evening and BE MY TRUE SELF.

For the first time I felt truly uninhibited. I walked around the office all morning wearing my new attire. When it was lunchtime The Architect called me to the viewing window that looked down on his basement sanctuary to discuss lunch.

As I walked into view The Architect dropped his pencil. His face turned green. He screamed, "*Noooooooooooooooooooo!*"

I instantly wondered had I put on the wrong tie. I turned and looked at myself in the mirror. The shirt and tie were correct, as was the trousers, the shoes, the glasses. My hair was identical to his. The fake boobs The Architect wore as a teenager fitted me like a glove. The fake butt looked good on me. The ball bag certainly made my package look bigger. The black jelly I attached to it was probably too much. Yes, that's probably it. Maybe I had gone too far?

I looked sideways and glanced at Momma's sewing machine, which I had rebuilt. Connected to the power socket. Connected to the steel rods. I took off the black jelly and mounted it just like The Architect's Momma like it.

I walked back to the viewing window. The Architect was still screaming, so I pressed mute on the audio from the basement. I could see The Architect continue to scream. But I could no longer hear him.

His voice. The voice of reason. Was not to be heard again today.

Just then the sun shone through the window on me. I glowed.

The world has a funny way of doing that. No one seems to know what pain you experienced yesterday. Because everyone is so preoccupied with today.

ABOUT THE BOOK

Amidst the integrity of world-class design and architecture, amidst the world of art and food, where money goes hand in hand with fame, in a world where corporations make and destroy people's lives, The Architect and his Assistant design homes. But not just homes. They design the crème de la crème of residential residences, and they punish the owners of their homes for crimes against good taste. They punish them for forgetting they cannot change even one thing in their homes. Not the color, not the door handle, not the doorstop. They punish them to within an inch of their lives.

ABOUT THE AUTHOR

After almost forty years in television and advertising, it was time to write a book. After having two screenplays optioned in Hollywood and having neither produced ... it was definitely time to write a book.

I have lived a wonderful life traveling the world and meeting some of the world's most talented, selfish, and bizarre characters.

I live with my wife and family an hour outside of Sydney by the beach.

25290794R00119

Made in the USA
Lexington, KY
25 August 2013